THE COURTNEY'S MYSTERIES AND ADVENTURES

Summer Beach Vacation

Timothy William Lawrence

DEDICATION

I would like to dedicate this novel to my precious little six-year-old granddaughter, Annalise Claire. She has been such a delight in my life and has filled my world with endless joy. We have the most extreme fun playing games, her playing dentist and hairdresser and so many other characters. I love you, sweet Lise!

TABLE OF CONTENTS

ACKNOWLEDGEMENTS

I would like to thank my precious wife of 42 years for her patience, wisdom, and support. She has endured much with this bonehead throughout our years together.

The Bible says in Proverbs 27:17, "As iron sharpens iron, so one person sharpens another."

Thanks to all those who have invested their time, given me constructive comments, driven me to be the best I could be, shared their wisdom, and continued to support me through the years. I'm a rich, rich man because of the relationships God has blessed me with.

INTRODUCTION

I began writing this novel in 1994. My wife, Vicki, and I had been given the joy of having an amazing daughter. Her name is Courtney. When Courtney was eight years old, her best friend's name was also Courtney, hence the basis of my first four novels.

I'm not sure why I waited so long to pick up my writing again and finish this first novel. The only reason I could give is that the timing was right. I've thoroughly enjoyed putting on paper past events and memories and turning them into novels. It's been quite therapeutic and extremely enjoyable.

I have been in the music ministry and student ministry since 1972. My primary purpose and prayer for publishing my novels are to help pre-teen young people to know that they have value and purpose. That God cares about them and everything they are involved in. I want them to know that He is that personal. In fact, so personal that He gave His only Son, Jesus Christ, to die for their sins so that they might experience eternal life and also enjoy a wonderfully rewarding life while on earth.

I hope you and your pre-teen child will enjoy reading about various adventures and mysteries the two Courtneys experience. May it be an encouragement to you, as a parent, to remember the serious responsibility we have in raising our children to be Godly, respectful, polite, and helpful to others. Everyone struggles from time to time with being completely truthful. It's so easy to fib a little to make ourselves look better or to keep us from getting in some trouble. But it is never the best solution in any given situation. Hopefully, "Truth and Lies" will help preteens realize that honesty IS always the best policy, even when it's the most difficult thing to do.

CHAPTER ONE: BEACH VACATION

"What a rush! Let's do it one more time before we go. Okay, Court?"

"I'm game, Coco."

They grabbed another rubber mat, and climbed to the top of the giant water slide at Sugar Sands, Alabama's best water park, Waterville. It was a really fun amusement location. It was a twenty-acre water park and amusement park created in 1986. Its waterpark attractions included seventeen water slides, a lazy river, a wave pool, Shrimp Boat Village, Wa-Wa World, and Flowrider. The amusement park attractions include the Nascart Go-Carts, Cannonball Run roller coaster, thirty-six holes of miniature golf, Trampoline Thing, Fun Depot kiddie rides, the Escape House, a large arcade, and, of course, the slide the girls just went down. It was called "The Viper." The park boasted that the slide was 250 feet tall and had a 45-degree downward fall. Whether that was true or not didn't matter to the Courtneys. They still loved every second of the thrill. They entered the separate water tubes, and the employee counted it down for them to push off and slide. One, two, three, go! The race was on. Both girls encountered sharp twists and turns down the slippery cylinders, and then, sploosh! They both entered the pool of water at the bottom of the slide simultaneously.

"Whew! That was so much fun. I hate that we have to leave." Courtney said.

"Yeah, me, too. But we gotta get ready for supper, and tonight we're going to Mikie's." "Woohoo! Our favorite restaurant down here." Courtney hollered.

"Yeah. I hope Anne is singing tonight with her band. Love her singing." Coco said.

Courtney Lawrence and Courtney Sims had been best friends since they were five. They were almost thirteen now. To minimize confusion, Courtney Lawrence was nicknamed Coco, while Courtney Sims simply went by Courtney. They never were your run-of-the-mill students who stayed inside watching TV shows and playing video games. They were always outside riding their bikes, goofing off in the park, playing in the woods, or exploring some new place. They seemed to always be on an exciting adventure. Currently, they were in Sugar Sands, AL. Their families had rented a condo and were vacationing together for the week. They hung out all the time together back in Jackson, Mississippi, where they lived, and this was a vacation they had planned since last year. They wanted to go earlier in the summer, but because of Tim's work schedule, they had to wait till August. Coco's dad was a hard worker but always tried his best to make time for family events. The three-story condo was right on the beach. The Lawrence and Sims families left the water park and returned to the condo to get cleaned up before they went to Mikie's.

"Girls, y'all look water-logged," Coco's dad said.

"Yeah, they look like water rats," Ralph, Courtney's dad, added.

"Maybe so, but we had a great time," Coco answered, and Courtney agreed.

"By the way, dad and Mr. Sims, why wouldn't you go with us to ride The Viper?"

Melinda answered before they had a chance.

"Honey, now you know they are up in age, and you just get a little scared of things like that as you get older."

"I didn't see you going with them either, Mrs. Sims," Ralph replied.

All of them giggled.

It took them about two hours to get ready to go out and eat since they only had two bathrooms. When they arrived, the waiting time for a table was an hour. Anne Isbell was a well-known local singer in the area, and Coco was so excited because tonight she was performing at Mikie's. She sang, accompanied by John Griff, who was an amazing guitarist. They performed many songs from the seventies, eighties, nineties, and other current songs. This made the wait tolerable. Coco hoped that she could sing as well as Anne one day. By the time they got seated, the basket of crackers and butter on the table were all devoured within minutes, which helped curb their appetites. The server brought them some complimentary rolls and butter and took their food and drink orders. The food was terrific, as always. On the way back, they stopped at the Wal-Mart to get some breakfast items. Ralph and Tim stayed in the SUV while Melinda, Vicki, and the girls went inside.

"Hey, mom, dad told me we might go looking for sand crabs when we get back to the condo and said to look for a couple of nets or buckets to catch them in. We're going to the sporting goods area to see if they have any."

Melinda looked to see Vicki's approval and told them it would be fine to meet them at the front in about ten minutes. The girls took off toward the sporting goods. They asked an employee in that area if he knew where they could find a bucket or net, and he pointed them in that direction.

"Here they are, Coco."

"Good. Let's grab two buckets and head to the cashier's area."

They arrived up front just about the same time as their mothers did. They checked out, got in the SUV, and returned to the condo. Ralph, Tim, and the girls headed down to the beach to do some crabbing while Melinda and Vicki opted to stay and watch Chip and Joanna Gaines on HGTV remodel another house in Waco, TX.

The girls got close to the beach's edge, holding their buckets, and Ralph and Tim holding flashlights to see the sand crabs. They were cute little things about two inches wide and three inches long. They had six legs, beady eyes, and two intimidating claws. They caught about seven in their buckets.

"Hey, what's going on over there?" Courtney asked.

They all walked toward the gathered group and found out they were watching Matthew Isbell, who was very well known in Sugar Sands and the fishing industry as the Bama Beach Bum. He was doing some night fishing with his family and a couple of friends of theirs. They were attempting to catch a shark. Ralph grabbed Tim by the shoulder and spoke out.

"I can't believe we're here with Matthew Isbell, the Bama Beach Bum."

"The what what?" Tim stared at Ralph like he was crazy.

"The Bama Beach Bum. Don't tell me you've never heard of him. He has one of the most popular YouTube fishing channels that I watch just about every day. His saltwater fishing vids are not only entertaining but extremely informative."

"Yeah, okay, Ralph. What is he? Like your celebrity idol or something?"

Ralph gave Tim a look like you wouldn't understand.

"Think we got one!" Matthew yelled out.

He ran to the pole he'd placed in the sand and pulled it out of its holder. It was a fight, for sure. He tugged, yanked, and jerked, and after nine or ten minutes of sweat and exhaustion, he had reeled in a four-foot gray and white baby blacktip shark with very intimidating razor-sharp teeth. Everyone was loving the moment and gathered around the shark.

"Check it out, Tim! The Bum caught a shark, and we were here to see it."

Tim just shook his head back and forth, not believing how Ralph was so intrigued.

"Let's get closer so I can meet him," Ralph told Tim.

"Meet the shark or the Bama Beach Bum?" Tim quipped.

Ralph rolled his eyes at Tim and shifted around some of the others who were watching. He finally got close enough and engaged in a conversation with Mr. Isbell.

"So, do you catch these often?" Ralph asked.

"Not very often, but I'm not normally fishing for them either."

"Well, I'm impressed. You struggled for quite a while."

"Yeah, they can wear you out."

The crowd began to disperse after watching the impressive catch. The Bama Beach Bum allowed those who wanted to touch the shark. Tim and the girls were able at that time to move up to where Ralph was.

"Where are you all from, and what brought y'all out tonight?" The Bama Beach Bum asked Ralph.

Courtney jumped in and said, "We were catching sand crabs."

"Hi there. Yeah, that can be a lot of fun. I'll take my five-year-old girl out occasionally to do that. She's over there with my wife. She loves to see how fast they can crawl."

Coco asked him, "Isn't that Anne Isbell? We heard her sing tonight at Mikie's."

"That's her," Matthew responded.

"She has a beautiful voice," Coco added.

"I think so, too," Matthew said with a smile.

Courtney interjected. "Can we touch the shark?"

"Sure, you can." They all did, and then the Bum said.

"Please excuse me, but I need to place this bad boy back into the water."

They stood and watched him pick the shark up and gently slid him in the water. Once it hit the water, it took off like a bolt of lightning.

Ralph said louder than he meant, "Dude! I'd love to try that sometime."

The Bama Beach Bum looked at Ralph and asked, "How long are y'all here?"

"This week. Leaving Saturday."

"Well, I tell you what. If you want to meet me here Thursday evening around 8:00 p.m., we might be able to make that happen."

"Are you kidding? That would be awesome."

"See y'all then." The Bama Beach Bum replied.

Anne's and Matthew's little girl ran up to Coco and said hi to them.

Coco bent down and said, "Well, hi there. My name is Coco."

Coco saw Anne walking toward them and felt it would be okay to interact with their daughter.

Coco continued, "What's your name?"

"My name is Annalise Claire."

"What a pretty name. Do they call you AC sometime?"

Annalise wasn't sure how to answer that. Anne introduced herself to Coco.

"She is not very shy. She loves meeting other people. I have to be careful when we go out. She talks to everyone, and unfortunately, in this world, you have to be incredibly careful."

"Yes, ma'am. I understand. I hope you were okay with me talking to her."

"Absolutely. I had my eye on Annalise the whole time and felt she would be safe with you." Coco then added. "We saw you earlier tonight at Mikies. You have such a beautiful voice."

"Well, thank you very much. I heard the other gentleman say you and your friend will be here for the week. I hope you have a wonderful time."

"Thank you, miss Anne. I'm sure we will."

At that, Anne and Annalise helped Matthew with his fishing gear and walked up to their truck.

Ralph, Tim, and the girls piled into the Sims SUV and headed back to their condo.

"What a way to start our week of vacation on the beach. Water park, Mikie's, and seeing the Bama Beach Bum catch a black tip shark." Ralph excitedly spoke.

"Yeah, Ralph, I thought for sure you were going to give the Bum a big hug and tell him you were his biggest fan."

"Okay, Timothy. Enough out of you unless you want me to tell the girls about the time you met A. J. McCarron."

"Who's that, dad?" Courtney inquired.

"He played quarterback for the University of Alabama and even took them to two consecutive national championships in 2012 and 2013."

Coco asked Courtney's dad. "Mr. Ralph, tell us the story."

"Well, he and I had a pass to go to one of the football team's practices in Tuscaloosa and then went to Baumhower's to eat afterward. Guess who came in the front door but A.J. McCarron. Your dad went crazy. He jumped from his seat, introduced himself, and asked for his autograph. The whole time we were eating, he kept looking at the napkin with A.J.'s autograph."

"So, Courtney, I guess both of our dads have celebrity idols. You think we should tell our moms about this?"

The girls laughed, and Ralph and Tim just looked at each other and rolled their eyes.

All four walked into the condo's front door, and immediately, Vicki and Melinda told them to hush. They were engrossed in a love story they had found on TV. So, the four of them went downstairs and played some pool—Tim and Coco against Ralph and Courtney. After the best of five games, which Tim and Coco won, Melinda and Vicki came downstairs with a couple of bowls of popcorn, drinks, and brownies. The men and girls showed their appreciation by not leaving any leftovers.

"Mom," Coco called her mom, "did you know that dad had a celebrity idol with A.J. McCarron?"

"Oh yeah, and mom," Courtney called her mom, "did you know that dad had a celebrity idol with the Bama Beach Bum?"

Tim and Ralph looked at their daughters and then at their wives and finished their colas.

Vicki went first. "Well, honey, I knew he almostcried when I accidentally threw away the napkin with A. J.'s autograph on it."

Then, Melinda asked, "The Bama what what?"

"The Bama Beach Bum. We met him tonight when we were looking for sand crabs."

"Hmm, not sure I knew this about your dad. We might have to have a little talk."

"So, tell us, boys, Vicki continued the questioning, is this a problem, or do you two have this potential problem under control."

"Yeah," Melinda chimed in. Do you two need to go to a counselor for some help?"

The snickers started with all the females, and then Ralph and Tim joined in full laughter. It was pretty late, and they all decided it would be a suitable time to go to bed.

Even on vacation, the Sims and the Lawrences tried to make it a habit of going somewhere for a Sunday church service. They found a small church called City Hope. It was a contemporary setting and seemed to have a very friendly congregation. The worship service started at 10:30, and Coco couldn't believe it; for that matter, neither could Ralph. Anne Isbell was on stage with the praise team leading worship, and her husband, the Bama Beach Bum, was playing the bass guitar. Anne sang a solo with the praise team, and the song was 'The Blessing,' one of Coco's favorites. After twenty minutes of amazing worship in song, the young pastor stood up and shared from the Gospel of Luke, chapter fifteen. Normally, when people speak about this narrative, they refer primarily to the son who left his father, took his inheritance, and came back completely broke and humiliated.

The pastor took the story down a totally different path, which was very interesting. He spoke from the individual's perspective that had met the son when he had money and then their viewpoint when he had lost it all. He discussed how people can be very fickle and listed a few ways they show that. They will like you for what you can give them. They will like you as long as they can gain notoriety by knowing you. They will like you as long as you believe what they believe. They will like you as long as you don't confront them with the truth. He went on to speak to the congregation's believers, challenging them to stay the course and not let the world lead them astray. To live so differently that those who need Jesus will see Him in the way you live, and they will desire Him as Lord. Thirty-five minutes later, the pastor closed in prayer. As the people were leaving, Anne called out to Coco.

"Coco, was it?"

"Yes, ma'am."

"It's so good to see you and your friends here today. Looking at Courtney, she continued, what is your name?"

"Courtney, and, by the way, your singing is amazing."

"Thank you for the sweet comment."

Ralph had made a bee line to Matthew, the Bama Beach Bum, to tell him he was looking forward to Thursday evening. Matthew mentioned he was, too.

When the Lawrences and the Sims got into the car, Melinda said,

"So, that's your celebrity idol, huh?"

They all laughed except for Ralph. He just rolled his eyes and kept on driving. They stopped at Culver's to eat, and boy, was it crowded, but they made certain they ate there. It was one of their favorite places to dine. They ordered their food, found some seats, and waited for their name to be called to pick up their food. Ralph and Tim went to the front counter while the girls stayed seated. Tim tapped Ralph on the shoulder.

"You're not gonna believe this."

"What?" Ralph answered.

"Look who's coming through the side entrance."

There was the Isbells. They had come to eat at Culver's, too.

As soon as Matthew saw Ralph and Tim, he jokingly said, "Ralph, are you two stalking me?" Ralph was caught off guard and stuttered around until Matthew told him he was just joking. Tim cackled and said to Matthew, "He probably would, though. I think he wants to be just like you, Matt."

Mathew chuckled. "Man, is it ever busy today. Don't know if we'll find a seat."

At that moment, the family next to the Sims and Lawrences were leaving. Ralph told Matthew they could hold the seats next to them if they wanted to sit next to them. Matthew said that would be great. Ralph and Tim brought their own food to their table, and shortly after that came the Isbells with their food. They all enjoyed a fun time getting to know each other better and also eating Culver's cuisine, which was always very tasty.

"We better give up our tables. Tim said. "There are a lot of people needing them."

"Yep. We enjoyed the time, y'all. Thanks for letting us sit with you."

Ralph jumped in and said, "It was our pleasure. See you Thursday."

In the parking lot, Matthew leaned over to Tim and Ralph and asked them to hold up for a moment because he had something to mention.

"Hey, guys, I didn't want to alarm your family, but I thought it would be smart for you two to know."

Tim and Ralph listened intently to what the Beach Bum had to say.

"There has been a rash of break-ins during the summer and primarily in vacation condos on the beach. The authorities haven't gotten any real leads yet, but they think it's possibly teenagers or college kids. Just thought I'd inform you so you would be extra careful."

Ralph answered, "Really appreciate the heads up, Matthew. We'll stay vigilant and tell our wives, as well."

"Yeah, thanks, Matt," Tim added.

They all said their goodbyes and left Culvers. That night, they all gathered in the den and watched one of their favorite movies, 'The Railway Children.' After that, they all went to bed and got a great night's sleep.

Everyone slept a little later than a typical Monday morning. Melinda and Vicki got up and fixed some bacon, eggs, and biscuits. The smell was incredible and brought the rest of the crew to the kitchen to enjoy breakfast.

"Thank you so much, ladies, for cooking this morning." Tim offered.

Everyone else agreed with a nod and a grunt.

"What are we doing today?" Courtney asked.

Ralph responded that he didn't think anything was really planned.

"Can me and Courtney go to the beach later?"

Both sets of parents nodded in agreement that they could and just be sure to check in now and then and be safe.

Jokingly, Coco said to her mom, "Aww, mom. We were hoping to go parasailing and do some scuba diving with the sharks. You take all the fun out of everything."

"Oh, I'll take the fun out of everything, young lady. You better watch yourself."

They all chuckled. After eating breakfast, both Courtneys put on their bathing suits, got their masks and snorkels, and walked downstairs to the beach.

"I hope we can find something really cool in the water today," Courtney said.

"Me, too. Let's get in."

The girls stepped into the water, and it was a perfect temperature. They donned their masks and snorkels and dove into the water, which was a little cloudy and murky for whatever reason. They stayed close together as they explored the bottom of the gulf floor, hoping to find something interesting. One would see them on top of the water and then under the water, looking for something extraordinary. Every now and then, they would find some small seashells, a few fish, and some seaweed, but nothing out of the ordinary. As they continued their search, Courtney found a baby's pink shoe, and Coco found a child's sand shovel. They both came up to the top of the shallow water and stood talking to each other about the lack of valuables they were finding when they suddenly started yelling out that their legs were getting stung.

"Ow! Coco spoke out just about the same time Courtney did.

"What is stinging our legs, Coco?"

"I don't know, but let's get out of the water now."

The more they tried to swim away, the more they got entangled with whatever was stinging them, and both were having an exceedingly difficult time getting out of the water. Both girls screamed loudly and couldn't maneuver themselves out of the water because they seemed almost paralyzed.

A couple of young men heard them and saw the struggle they were involved in and swam out to help them. They grabbed each girl and dragged them back to the shore. As they lay on the sand, Courtney said.

"I'm really hurting."

"Me, too. It's even hard to breathe right now." Coco replied.

"The best way immediately for you two to get some relief is to rub and scrub the gulf water on your legs. The salt in it will help relieve the pain and will assist in getting the toxins out. Are you two alright with us doing that for you?"

Both girls nodded their heads, and the two men started the process.

As they rubbed, whelps started appearing, and one of the men spoke to them.

"You two were apparently surrounded by a group of jellyfish called the Portuguese Man O' War. They float in clusters in the water and are not intentionally trying to sting people in the water. They have exceptionally long tentacles, and once they come in contact with something or someone, their tentacles give out a poison that can cause various symptoms like nausea, a paralyzing effect, and even welts and swelling for a day or so. It takes a while for the poison to get extracted from the infected area, making the experience extremely uncomfortable, to say the least. Are you feeling any better, or is it still painful?" The young man asked.

Coco responded. "I can breathe better, but the stinging is still there."

"Yeah, same here. I can see the welts on me and Coco." Courtney replied.

One of the young men asked the girls, "Do you have any family close by we can reach for you?" Courtney pointed to their condo and told them their parents were there. The other young man said he'd go get them. It wasn't long before the girls saw Tim and Ralph running toward them with Melinda and Vicki close behind.

"Girls, are you okay?" Tim inquired.

Coco answered, "Yes sir, but the stinging just won't let up."

Courtney added, "It really hurts, Dad."

"I'm sorry, Court."

"Hi, we're their parents. What happened?"

One of the young men responded, "They got surrounded by a group of jellyfish called the Portuguese Man O' War. They don't intend any harm, but it can be very painful if you get in contact with their tentacles. We've been rubbing their legs with the gulf water, and that should help, but they'll need some Aloe vera gel and/or vinegar. Those two products will assist in relieving the pain."

"How do you two know this?"

"We're actually pre-med students at the University of Alabama in Birmingham and are down here for a little break."

Ralph interjected.

"Well, we're sure glad you two came to their rescue. Thank you." Melinda spoke up.

"Let's get the girls back to the condo. I've got some Aloe vera we can use."

"Yeah, and there's some vinegar in the kitchen cabinet," Vicki added.

The dads picked up their respective daughters and told the young men again how much they appreciated helping Coco and Courtney.

"We were glad to help. We hope they'll be fine." One of the young men answered.

Courtney and Coco were doing better after the spaghetti supper, but both still had a little higher than average temperature and continued to feel the stingers from the jellyfish.

"I think I'm going to bed," Courtney said with a yawn.

"I'm gonna do the same," Coco replied.

They slowly walked up to the third floor, put on their pajamas, brushed their teeth, and slipped into their beds.

"Hey, did you notice the Spongebob tattoo on that guy's ankle?" Coco asked.

"No. Spongebob? Really?"

"Yeah, I know, but it was definitely Spongebob. Maybe he's a fan."

"Maybe so. Kind of crazy, though. Courtney answered. Sure, hope we feel better in the morning."

"Me, too, Court. Why don't we say a quick prayer for each other."

"Sounds great. I'll go first. Courtney replied. Father, thank You for the day You gave us to enjoy. We're hurting with these crazy, stingy things, and we pray that You will help us get better quickly. In Your name, Jesus. Amen"

Coco was next. "Lord, I ask the same thing, and also, please bless the two guys who helped us today. Thank You for sending them there at the right time. We love You, Jesus. Amen. Night, Coco."

"Night. Court."

CHAPTER TWO: BREAK IN

Tuesday morning arrived, and the Courtneys slept fairly well. The scuffling around by Courtney's parents woke the girls up. Melinda and Vicki thought they heard the girls talking, so they decided to go upstairs and check on the girls.

"How are you two feeling this morning?" Vick asked.

Courtney was the first to answer. "I feel a little sick in my stomach and can still feel a stinging in my legs, but I'm okay."

"Yeah, about the same as Courtney. It's just an uncomfortable feeling. Coco added.

"Well, we're sorry that this happened to you two. Hopefully, you two will feel completely better by tomorrow. We're making some breakfast sandwiches. Would you like us to bring you one? Both thanked their moms and said they would come down to get one in a few moments.

"What a bummer! Coco said. On vacation, and this had to happen."

"Really! Courtney answered. I guess it will give us some time to catch up on a couple of movie series we've been wanting to binge-watch."

"Yeah. Let's go get one of those sandwiches."

They slowly slipped out of bed and traversed downstairs where their parents were.

"Good morning, you two. Ralph spoke. How are you two feeling?"

"I hope with their hands, Ralph." Tim quipped.

Everyone gave him a loud sigh for the bad joke. Melinda, in her usual manner, fluttered her eyelids at Tim. This was her normal trademark reaction whenever Tim told one of his 'dad' jokes.

"We're okay." Coco said. "Still hurting with the stinging feeling."

"Sorry, ladies." Tim said. "We're praying that it all gets better real soon."

"Thanks, Dad."

"Girls, me and Vicki are going to Wal-Mart later to get some items. Is there anything you want?" Melinda asked.

"How about some chocolate milk?" Coco asked.

Before the ladies could answer, Courtney chimed in with, "Yeah, and maybe a couple of honey buns? I've heard from world-renowned authorities that those two items were the best remedy for jellyfish stings."

"Oh, really. Well, I guess we'll have to get them then. What do you think, Melinda?"

"Oh, of course."

They all chuckled.

Right before Melinda and Vicki got into their vehicle, Courtney ran to the front door and asked them to get more Aloe Vera. They said they were going to do that. The girls went back upstairs and started playing Dots and Boxes on their cell phones in their third-story room while their dads were downstairs playing pool on the bottom floor. Ralph had just received a notification on his phone that the Bama Beach Bum would be near their area doing some fishing. "Hey, Tim. I just found out that 3-B is gonna be fishing near us in about fifteen minutes." Tim asked.

"3-B? What is that?"

"The Bama Beach Bum. Come on, Tim. Get with it."

Tim rolled his eyes and said, "Yeah, I guess we could go see him as long as you don't run up and give him a big hug." Tim laughed. "I wonder what he's gonna be fishing for today?"

"Doesn't matter. It's just fun being there, watching him. I'm gonna bring my fishing gear, too." "Oh, wait. Tim interjected. The girls. What about them?"

"They'll be fine. Tell them where we're going and call us if they need anything."

"Sounds like a plan," Tim responded.

While Ralph got his fishing gear together, Tim went upstairs and told the girls where they were going. The girls would have loved to have joined them, but they still weren't feeling totally up to par. Better, but not totally well yet.

"Alright, love you two. We'll see you later." Tim said.

He left the room and headed downstairs.

"We'll holler if we need y'all for anything," Coco yelled at them as they left.

Courtney was looking at their various video games and challenged Coco.

"Hey, let's play Bump It Up. We haven't played that in a while."

"Well, if you want another beat down, okay." Coco quipped.

"Sounds like a challenge. Let's do this!" Courtney quipped back.

They donned their headphones and began.

While driving around the beach area, the one driving said.

"I think it's time we make a doctor's visit to our little patients and see how they're doing." "Huh?" the other one said.

"You know. The little punks we pulled out of the water that got stung by the jellyfish."

"Why would we do that?"

"You know what, Robbie? I think when brains were being given out, you thought they said rain, and you went inside so you wouldn't get wet. We'll go there pretending to care about their wellness, but while there, we'll check out the place to see what they have that's worth takin' so if we get a chance to break in later when they're out." "Oh, I get it now." Steve just shook his head at Robbie.

The two pre-med students parked in the driveway and walked upstairs to the condo's front door, where the Sims and Lawrences were staying. Steve knocked a few times, but no one answered. Steve turned the door handle and discovered the door was unlocked.

"What a piece of luck. He opened it and called out. Hi. Is anyone here? Just wanted to stop by and see how the girls were doing."

No answer. They cautiously stepped inside and looked around. It appeared to be empty.

After twenty minutes or so of extreme dueling and some close-scoring games, the girls decided to go to the kitchen and grab something to drink. When they took off the headgear, they both looked at each other curiously. Courtney put her forefinger to her lips and whispered. "Did you hear that? I thought I heard someone downstairs."

Coco whispered back. "Me, too. It's probably our dads or moms."

"Our dads wouldn't be back this soon," Courtney said quietly.

The girls tip-toed to the front bedroom window and didn't see the Sim's SUV, but they did see two mountain bikes. They both heard someone coming up the stairs. Courtney nodded at Coco, motioning for them to get under the bed. It was a tight squeeze, but they finally slid under as stealthily as possible and just in the nick of time.

Their bedroom door opened, and they could see two sets of feet and legs walking around, but they couldn't see their faces. In fact, one of them got so close that they could see the Spongebob tattoo on the ankle Coco saw on one of them yesterday.

"Nothin' in here is worth getting. One of the men said. It must be where those stupid girls sleep. You can smell the Aloe Vere and vinegar for a mile. Let's go to the other rooms."

They walked throughout the condo as the Courtneys nervously listened and remained as quiet as possible.

"Are these the guys that helped us this week? What are they doing here?" Coco softly asked.

"I don't know, Coco. Do you think they're the ones who have been breaking into the condos?" They both looked at each other in panic and fear and continued to listen.

One of the men spoke from the second-floor bedroom where the Sims' parents slept.

"I don't know if this jewelry is worth anything, but Al can tell us at the pawn shop."

The other one mentioned, "In the other bedroom, I grabbed some change that was on the nightstand, and this iPad is pretty sweet. I might just keep it for myself."

The first guy then said, "Robbie, you truly are an idiot. You can't take that. It can be tracked. Leave it. Come on. Let's get out of here before the family returns."

When they got to the den and kitchen area, Robbie looked in the fridge and asked the other guy. "Hey, they got Mountain Dews. The nectar of the gods. Yo, Steve. You want a Dew?"

"Nah. I'm good."

The other popped the top, downed a big swig, and set it down on the counter.

"I'm gonna see what kind of snacks they have. You want something?"

"No, and come on, Robbie. We'll get something later. We don't want to get caught."

"Okay, but you're buying."

He slammed the pantry door, took another huge gulp of the Mountain Dew, finished it off, and tossed the empty can into the den onto the couch. The girls heard the front door shut, and rushed to the window,making sure they weren't seen. They were riding mountain bikes and headed toward the main traffic light.

"Can you believe this? We gotta call our dads." Coco said.

She dialed her dad's cell and relayed to him what had just occurred. Ralph and Tim ran as fast as they could back to the condo.

"You two, okay?" Ralph asked frantically.

"We're okay, dad. It was just a little scary. We were in our bedroom under the bed the whole time." Coco replied.

Courtney added, "We couldn't see their faces, just their legs and feet. We heard them say they took some jewelry and some change from upstairs. One of them drank a Mountain Dew. That's probably it on the couch. We didn't touch it because we thought the police might be able to get some fingerprints off it."

"You did good, girls."

Ralph dialed 911. The desk Officer at the police station answered.

"Sugar Sands Police Station. Can I help you?"

Ralph told the Officer what had occurred, and he was connected to Officer Graham within minutes. He told Ralph that he and another Officer would swing by their condo within an hour. It was only a few minutes, and they heard a couple of knocks on the condo's front door. Tim opened it and invited the Officers inside.

"I'm Chief Graham, and this is Officer Watson. We understand you called about a possible break-in and burglary."

Tim was quick to answer. "Yes, sir. While our wives were out shopping and we were fishing, our daughters were upstairs playing some video games when they heard odd noises downstairs. They remained upstairs, hiding under their bed."

Officer Watson leaned in and asked the girls. "Ladies, were you able to see their faces?"

Courtney was quick to answer. "No, sir. We could only see their legs and feet."

Coco added. "But we did see that one of them had a Spongebob tattoo on their ankle. Earlier this week, my friend and I got stung by some jellyfish, and these two college students pulled us out of the water. One of them had a SpongeBob tattoo on their ankle.".

Ralph chimed in and spoke. "One of the young men ran here to our condo to tell us about our daughter's incident. We ran down to the beach and met them. They seemed very nice and extremely helpful. It would be hard to believe they were the ones who attempted a burglary here."

The Officer asked the girls to continue about the burgarly. Courtney and Coco riveted off as many details as they could remember as the Officers took notes on their notepads.

Coco told the officers they heard one of them say they could smell the Aloe Vera and vinegar that we had been using on our legs. They were the ones who told us to use it on our stings when they helped us on the beach."

"How did they know this was your condo?" Officer Watson asked, looking at Ralph and Tim.

Tim quickly answered, "One of the men who had helped our girls asked them where they could find their parents. The girls pointed to our condo, and one of them ran here and told us about our girl's injuries. We, of course, ran to the shore, thanked the two men, and carried our daughters back here to medicate their stings. As we were carrying our girls, the two young men told us to be sure to use Aloe Vera and vinegar. They seemed genuinely nice and sincere."

Officer Graham commented. "You may not have heard, but there has been a rash of break-ins and burglaries in various vacation condos along this track of the beach."

Ralph chimed in. "We heard that from Matthew Isbell just a few nights ago."

"The Bama Beach Bum! Really good guy. A local celebrity around here." Chief Graham mentioned.

Officer Watson looked at the girls and asked, "Was there anything they touched that you know of?"

Courtney answered. "Yessir. The Mountain Dew can over there on the couch."

Coco added. "We left it there and didn't touch it. We thought you might get some fingerprints off of it."

" Brilliant girls, you two have here."

Tim and Ralph both gave a slight smile. Officer Watson bagged the can in a plastic bag.

"Do you always leave your front door open?" Chief Graham asked.

"No, sir. We think that one of the girls forgot to lock it back after they called out to their moms to get them some more Aloe Vera before they drove away."

"Makes sense. Try to be more careful about that, girls." Chief Graham encouraged.

Both girls responded with a nod and a yessir.

"We appreciate the call. Hopefully, we can catch these two very soon. If the two men helped your girls, then at least they can be pulled out of a lineup. You all have a good night, and let us know if you think of anything else that would be useful."

"Thank you, Officers. We appreciate what you're doing. Stay safe." Ralph said.

Coco then spoke loudly to get their attention. "Sir. We also heard one of them call the other Steve."

Courtney added. "That's right, and the other one was called Robbie."

"Thanks. That could be immensely helpful." Chief Graham answered with gratitude.

As the Officers were leaving, Vicki and Melinda almost ran into them.

Vicki cried out, "What has happened? Why are the police here?"

Melinda furiously asked. "Is everyone okay?"

"We're all fine. We just had a little incident happen while you two were gone." Ralph replied.

"What kind of little incident?" Vicki asked.

Tim answered and told them the whole story.

"You two call that little?" Melinda and Vicki commented at the same time.

Ralph responded. "Well, we didn't mean little, like it wasn't a big deal. We meant little, as in no one got hurt or anything like that."

Their wives looked at them with much irritation and asked where they were while this happened.

"Ralph got a notification that the Bama Beach Bum was going to be doing some shore fishing a couple of condos down, so we thought we would go see him."

The ladies then asked what the police said they would do about the break-in.

Tim answered, "They took a Mountain Dew bottle that one of the young men drank. They're hoping to find some fingerprints. Other than that, they would continue to be on the lookout."

"We're glad you two are okay," Melinda said to Coco and Courtney.

Vicki and Melinda went upstairs to investigate whose jewelry the men had taken. It ended up being a couple of pieces of costume jewelry of Melinda's. She bought it at Wal-Mart a day or two before they left for their trip. She liked the jewelry, but it didn't have much value.

Once things settled down from the excitement, Vicki asked, "The menu for tonight called for taco salad. How does it sound to everybody?"

The whole bunch made motions that said that sounded yummy. Melinda asked the girls if they were feeling any better, and both Courtneys said they were much better. Every now and then, they would feel a sting or some discomfort, but other than that, they were fine. Melinda tossed her daughter the Aloe Vera they had bought, and Courtney took it upstairs. About an hour later, they all gathered at the table to chow down, grabbed hands, prayed for the food, and thanked the Lord for protecting the girls and that the two guys would get caught soon.

Supper was terrific, and after everything was cleaned up and put away, they decided to have a game night. They started with 'Left, Center, Right.' It was one of the girl's favorites. Then, they all played a silly game that Ralph and Tim made up. At least Vicki and Melinda thought it was silly. The girls loved it. The wives were a team, the dads were a team, and the Courtneys were a team. They would take three couch pillows between them, and each team at a time had to maneuver from the designated starting place to a specified area without touching the floor because it was pretend lava. The pillows were their only protection. The team that made it to the location the fastest was the winner.

They took a break, got some Pillsbury homemade chocolate chip cookies and milk, and then brought out the game Quirkle. It was a crowd-pleaser, as well. They played for an hour or so, and it was getting late, so they decided to go to bed. Courtney and Coco had just gotten into their beds when Courtney asked Coco a curious question.

"Hey, Coco. What would you have done if those guys had found us under our bed?"

"Wow, Court. I really haven't thought about it. That's creepy to think about. What would you have done?" Coco countered.

Courtney briefly thought and then said, "Well, I would have jerked from his hold on me and given the first one a roundhouse kick upside the head. I would have then spun around and thrown a side kick into the stomach of the other one. That would have given us both time to run down and out of the condo."

"Hmm, well, miss Karate Kid, I feel safer knowing you're with me."

They chuckled and were truly thankful that the guys didn't see them. Before they went to sleep, they prayed and thanked the Lord for His protection and that those two would get caught very soon.

CHAPTER THREE: EXPLORING SUGAR SANDS AND MEETING NEW FRIENDS

Wednesday morning began with the fantastic smell of cinnamon toast. Tim, Coco's dad, was the king of making cinnamon toast, but this time, he was using some homemade bread that Melinda and Vicki found at a local store. All the family members were in the kitchen, savoring the rich aroma of butter, sugar, and cinnamon. Ralph told all the females to have a seat at the table and he would get the plates and napkins. He took everyone's order of what they wanted to drink. The adults got their coffee fix, and the girls got their chocolate milk fix. On the way to the kitchen table, Vicki walked by Tim and looked at his delicacies.

"Oh, my goodness, Tim. You'll give us all a heart attack with so much butter and sugar!"

Ralph submitted. "Yeah, but what a way to go."

Melinda looked at him and gave him her patented fluttering eyelids look.

Tim replied to Vicki, "Well, babe, I'll eat yours if you don't want your slice of heaven."

"Oh no. I'm getting mine."

They were scrumptious. "Tim, you outdid yourself."

"Well, thank you, Ralph. And might I add? You did a fabulous job handing out the plates and taking the drink orders."

Melinda quipped, "Maybe you two might find a job working at a diner if you ever lose your current jobs."

Vicki and the girls got tickled at her remark, while Ralph and Tim ignored them.

Vicki added with a smirk, "Cleaning up is also a part of restaurant work, which you two might need some practice with, so thank you, boys, for cleaning up while we women retire over here to the den."

Tim and Ralph didn't take long to clean the kitchen and join the ladies.

"What's the plan for today?" Coco asked.

The adults looked at each other, and Melinda said, "Nothing really. We thought we could just hang out here and relax. Vic and I had talked about going to the pool, too."

"Boring!" Courtney moaned.

"Really. Coco agreed. Hey, can me and Court go bike riding up the strip?"

Again, the parents looked at each other, and Tim answered.

"Sure, that should be okay. Just please be sure to be careful. Stay as far off the road as you can."

The Courtneys nodded that they would.

Ralph added, "Hey girls, if Melinda, Vicki, and Tim are okay with this, we'll meet you two at Jungle Jack's mini golf and arcade around noon. After playing putt-putt golf, We can eat some pizza across the street at Paparazzio's.

"The girls loved the idea, and the other parents unanimously agreed.

"Come on, Court. Let's get out of our pajamas, put some other clothes on, and go riding."

"Right behind you, Coco."

The girls got ready in record time. They had been cooped up long enough and couldn't wait to explore the city while they tooled around on their bicycles.

"Be sure to put on some sunscreen, you two." They heard Vicki yell.

And in unison, the girls yelled back. "Yes, ma'am."

After applying the sunscreen, the girls told their parents they would meet them at noon at Paparazzio's. The parents reminded them to be careful and that they would see them there.

There was a slight overcast, which made their bike riding that much more enjoyable. They had ridden all the way to the Hangout restaurant. They turned left and went up Highway 59, which was in the direction of Papazzio's. There weren't as many vehicles to be worried about since it was the middle of the week, but they were still very cautious and aware of their surroundings. They stopped and parked their bikes at Alvin's, a beach store with everything a vacationer needed. They went inside, goofed off, and were about to get back on their bikes when they noticed a young black girl standing beside her. In Courtney fashion, she looked at the girl and spoke.

"Hi. My name is Coco, and this is Courtney. What's your name?"

It caught the girl slightly off guard, but then she replied, "Keisha."

"We're from Jackson, Mississippi. Coco mentioned.

"I'm from Montgomery, Alabama. Me and my parents are here for the week. They had to go to Wal-Mart to get some things and said it would be okay if I rode my bike around as long as I didn't go too far."

"You're welcome to hang out with us if you want. We're just riding around and doing some exploring." Courtney commented.

"That would be great. I was getting pretty bored, to be honest. Here are my mom and dad pulling in right now. I'll ask them."

They stepped out of their car, and Keisha introduced her new friends to them. Keisha's mom was a petite, small-framed lady, and her dad was easily 6' 5". After the introduction, she asked if she could hang out with them.

Keisha's mom looked at her husband and asked him what he thought. They both agreed it would be fine.

Coco mentioned to the Bradfords, "Later, we were going to join our parents at Jungle Jack's mini golf and arcade and then eat at Paparazzio's Pizza. Why don't you all join us? We could call our parents, and we know they wouldn't mind."

Before the Bradfords could respond, Courtney had already dialed her mom's cell and told her the whole story.

"My mom asked if she could talk to you, Ms. Bradford. Her name is Melinda."

A little caught off guard, Ms. Bradford took Courtney's cell.

"Hi, Melinda. This is Cindy."

"Hi, Cindy. Courtney told me how they met your daughter, you and your husband, and we would love for you all to join us later if you'd like."

Cindy looked at Keisha's dad, Silas, and told him about the invite. They both told Melinda they would love to meet them today.

"Great! We'll see you all at Jungle Jack's mini golf and arcade at noon. Melinda said. By the way, we're eating at Paparazzio's afterward. Please feel free to eat with us, too."

"Sounds like fun, Melinda. We look forward to meeting you all."

Cindy gave Courtney's cell back to her.

"Mom, dad. Is it okay to ride my bike to Jungle Jack's with Coco and Courtney?"

"Sure, just be careful."

"Okay. Love y'all." Keisha replied.

All three girls pedaled away, heading north on Highway 59. They stopped at the small overpass that overlooked a real marshy area and happened to spot an alligator sunning in the water.

"Cool! Check it out." Keisha pointed toward the large reptile with its snout and eyes sticking out of the water. "An Alligator!"

"Whoa! Coco and Courtney screamed in excitement.

After viewing the beast for a few minutes, they reconvened their riding and rode to the Sugar Sands Zoo. It would not be there much longer because they were moving to another location. It was always a favorite place to visit, and seeing Patti Hall, the zoo director, was always a pleasure. It was getting closer to noon, and they traveled toward Jungle Jack's.

"I'm so glad we three got together. This is so much fun. Keisha commented.

"We agree totally!" Coco and Courtney said.

There was not a sidewalk that the girls could traverse, so they had to dodge some careless drivers and were careful as they whipped in and out of the various store's parking lots. At one point, a driver in a truck pulled right in front of them at a Dollar General store, causing the girls to stop on a dime. The truck missed hitting them by a couple of feet. Courtney and Keisha continued riding their bikes, but Coco didn't. They looked back, and Courtney asked her, "What are you doing, Coco?"

"Hold on." She replied.

Courtney noticed her looking quite intently at the truck, and she also turned her direction there. Two men stepped out, and it was the pre-med students.

"That's the guys, Coco." Courtney said excitedly.

"I know. I recognized them as soon as they stepped out of their truck. Come on."

Coco rode closer to the truck to get their license plate number.

"Coco, be careful. They don't need to spot us."

"I know. Coco responded. Bummer! No plates. That figures. At least we know the truck make is a Tacoma."

"Who are they?" Keisha asked.

"We'll tell you later, but right now, we need to get out of here before they come out of the store and spot us."

The girls dug in their heels, pedaled as fast as they could, and finally arrived at Jungle Jack's parking lot at about 12:30.

The girl's parents had already introduced themselves to each other and were talking up a storm like a bunch of old friends at a school reunion.

Tim spoke first. "Coco, Courtney, didn't we say we'd meet you two at noon?"

"Yessir, Coco answered, but we had a slight interruption, dad. Well, next time, call and let us know when you'll be late."Both girls answered, "Yessir."

"So, what was the interruption?" Ralph asked.

Courtney asked him if they could tell him later.

"Females! Always so secretive." Ralph quipped, not knowing the seriousness of the reason.

Melinda looked at the other girl. "You must be Keisha."

"Yes, ma'am." Keisha shyly nodded.

"Your parents tell us you are also going into the seventh-grade next year."

"Yes, ma'am."

"Well, I'm sure you're looking forward to it as much as the girls are."

"Thanks for inviting Keisha to hang out with y'all. She was getting pretty bored with us old people." Keisha's mom commented to Courtney and Coco.

"We're glad, too. We've had a lot of fun today." Courtney replied.

Vicki jumped in and said, "I'm ready for some putt-putt golf competition. Just to remind everyone, I am the reigning champ from the last time we played."

Silas quipped back, "Oh, trash-talking already. Well, Vicki, it's only fair to tell you that I've never been beaten at mini golf with my immediate family or extended one, for that matter."

Ralph spoke up, "All talk and no action. Let's let the golfing do the talking."

They all laughed and headed to Jungle Jack's entrance. After paying and getting their golf clubs and different painted balls, the game was on. It ended up that Melinda beat everybody, and she was the least athletic of all. With her famous fluttering of her eyes and holding up her club, she said to them all.

"Did I beat Vicki, the reigning champ, and the one and only Silas? Who would have ever thought it?"

That got a fair round of chuckles.

Cindy said, "If I'm not mistaken, Melinda, the winner buys lunch."

Melinda tipped her head downward, looked over her glasses, and gave Cindy a look that said, "I don't think so."

They all chuckled.

The Sugar Sands Parkway was always too busy to cross on foot, so they all piled into separate vehicles and drove across the street. The aroma of the pizza was fantastic. They found a table for nine, ordered their pizza, and patiently waited. Courtney asked her dad to wait so she could talk to him. He did, and she told him the reason they were late.

"Court, why didn't you tell us that before we played golf?"

"I wasn't sure if I should say anything in front of Keisha's parents. I'm sorry, dad."

"No, no, you probably did the right thing. They didn't see you girls, did they?"

"No sir, at least we don't think so."

"What kind of vehicle were they in?"

"A white Tacoma."

"Did y'all get the license plate?"

"No, sir. They didn't have one."

"Well, at least we know what kind of vehicle they're driving. I'll call the police station right now."

Ralph called the number that he put into his cell phone earlier. He told the girls to go back to the table.

The desk Officer answered. "Sugar Sands Police Station. Can I help you?"

Ralph asked for Officer Watson or Chief Graham, but neither was in, so Ralph left an informative message and asked the desk Officer to get one of them to give him a call. Ralph walked back to the table, saw the curiosity on everyone's faces, and decided to explain to Cindy and Silas what had happened and then gave an update on what the girls had seen earlier.

"We heard some folks at our condo where we're staying talking about recent break-ins. We've been sure to lock down everything before we leave our building." Silas said.

"This is a little unnerving, to say the least," Cindy commented.

"It really is. Maybe the police knowing the type of vehicle will help a little." Melinda added.

The pizza couldn't have come any sooner. They were all claiming to be starving to death.

"Nothing like an all-meat pizza," Silas said.

"You'd be right there, Silas," Tim answered.

"Sure, glad we got two larges. I believe we can down both of them."

"You can have all you want of that heart-stopper because this trash pizza with vegetables is going to be unbelievable," Melinda commented while grabbing a piece.

Vicki and Cindy agreed and did the same. The girls ordered a large pepperoni and were digging in simultaneously.

"Tim then said. "I think we forgot to thank the Lord for this mess."

"We sure did," Ralph responded. What are you waiting for, Tim?"

After Tim prayed, everyone continued the feast. The pizza was incredible, and the company was too. In fact, the new acquaintances got along so well that they decided to make another date for supper later in the week. As they were leaving the restaurant, Coco and Courtney asked their parents if Keisha could spend a couple of nights with them. They said it would be fine as long as it was okay with Keisha's parents. It was, and the girls couldn't have been more excited. They followed the Bradfords to the condo where they were staying to get Keisha some clothes for the next couple of days. Once they got her belongings, the Sims and Lawrence's drove to their condo.

"Wow! Right on the beach! And the view is awesome!" Keisha exclaimed.

Courtney responded. "Yeah, we like the balcony, too. It's fun to sit out there and watch people down below. Sometimes Coco and I will make up crazy stories about them."

"What do you mean?"

"Come on." Courtney waved at Keisha, and she followed her and Coco onto the balcony.

"Okay, let's see. See the couple with the two children?" Courtney asked.

"Yeah."

"Okay. Here's their story. The man is a banker, and his wife is a teacher. Their youngest child is six, and the other one is nine. The husband has just received a $38,000.00 bonus from the bank where he works. Little does he know that the police are in front of the building right now and are waiting in the parking deck to nab him and take him to jail. They do, and he claims he is innocent. His wife is confused and can't believe what is happening. Of course, both children are crying. After the investigation, the police discovered the man was telling the truth. He was innocent. One of the bank Officers had written him a check and told him it was a bonus when, in reality, the bank Officer was lying. He set the man up to make it look like he'd stolen the money. The bank Officer was attempting to get him fired because the husband had gotten the raise and position he thought he should get."

Courtney stopped spinning her pretend narrative. "Oh, I get it. Keisha said. Crazy is right. Just made-up stories for fun. You have quite an imagination, Courtney."

"Well, Courtney and I have been doing this on just about every vacation. It helps to kill the boredom that we run into occasionally." Coco mentioned.

Keisha then said, "Let me try one."

"Go for it, girl." Courtney and Coco replied.

"Alright, umm, see the woman all by herself next to the two umbrellas?"

Both Courtneys strained to see who Keisha was talking about, and then they spotted her.

"Yep." They said in unison.

"We'll she used to be an extremely popular movie star. She played in some really great movies with well-known actors like Denzel Washington, Alfre Woodard, Sally Fields, and Liam Neeson. She was also well known for leaving the movie set while making a film and wouldn't tell anyone where she was going or when she would return. One time, she left, at least that was what everyone thought, and she disguised herself as one of the hands in the film she was acting in. She said later that she did it to see what the director and other actors were saying about her. In fact, she heard them make such mean and irresponsible statements about her that she sued them for defamation. It's reported that she made close to $5,000,000. Since that happened, she had a tough time finding work. That's when she decided to start traveling the world. She got bored with that and decided she had to ramp up her life and start doing something exciting and challenging. She became a world-wide expert thief. She stole precious jewels from jewelry stores all over the world. Then, she upped her new lifestyle by stealing famous paintings. She was in Italy at the Louvre and was going to steal one of the most famous paintings of all time. The Mona Lisa. She planned her scheme out perfectly with one hick-up. The night before, she had a little too much to drink, and she mentioned to a person she was drinking with her plan. That individual happened to work for the Italian police department as one of their secretaries. The Italian police were ready and waiting the next night and caught her red-handed. She spent 30 years in jail, and now you can find her at various stateside locations where she would never be recognized.

"Oh, my goodness, Keisha. That was so believable. You've done this before." Coco said with amazement.

"No, never have, but I have always had a highly active imagination. My mom told me when I played with my first doll at age two, I gave her the name of Abigail, and she was a nurse, then a teacher, then, believe it or not, an astronaut."

They all chuckled at that.

"Okay, Coco. Your turn." Keisha pushed.

"Well, I don't know if I want to go after you. Mine will be pathetic after your incredible story, but I'll give it a try."

Before Coco could start her fictitious narrative, her mom hollered from downstairs. "Didn't think you three would want any, but we thought we'd ask anyway. We just finished making some fresh homemade brownies and have some Bluebell ice cream to go on top." The girls almost ran over each other, coming down the stairs.

"Thanks a lot, Vicki. Me and Tim wanted them all for ourselves. Now we gotta share them with these little brats." Ralph jokingly said loud enough for the girls to hear.

"Dad, you don't need it anyway. Just look at your belly." Courtney replied.

"Girl, I'm proud of my six-pack," Ralph commented.

"It looks more like a keg," Melinda added.

All of them snickered. The Courtneys and their newfound friend savored every bite, and so did the adults.

"Thanks a lot," the girls said as they returned to their third-story room.

"Alright, Coco. We're waiting." Keisha pressed.

They went out on the balcony, and Coco looked around. She finally eyed the character she would star in her make-believe story.

"See the young girl standing by herself right outside the pool?"

Courtney and Keisha both nodded their heads.

"She's a runaway. She's only seventeen. She's from New Orleans, Louisiana, and her name is Ophelia. She had a great life with a family that seemed extremely happy. They would go out to eat, see a movie, and shop. They were also earnest about their church life. They went every Sunday together. Her mom and dad would even have a devotion each night in her bedroom. And then, when she was nine years old, her momma left her daddy for another man. In fact, the man was the assistant pastor of the church they were attending. It broke her daddy's heart entirely in two. Her mom never came back to see him or Ophelia. Her daddy started drinking, and then he even began using drugs. He'd go to the casino with any money he had left and lose all of it. Obviously, he was trying to find something to fill the void left by his wife. He finally lost his job at the boat docks, and his relationship with his daughter worsened. She tried to get him to go back to church, but with what happened, he said he'd never step into another church as long as he lived. One day, Ophelia came home from school, and her daddy wasn't there, and he never came home. She never saw her dad or mom again.

By this time, she was fifteen and decided to move away. She lived in Pascagoula, Mississippi, for a year. She lied about her age and was able to get work at a Huddle House as a server. She started a relationship with one of her co-workers, which was a huge mistake. He used her for whatever he could get out of her and then kicked her out of his trailer. After working at the Huddle House and living on the streets, she decided to take up roots and travel again. Mobile, Alabama, was her next stop. She was able to find work at a Waffle House as a cook. She made enough money to rent a small rundown apartment by the docks by working double shifts. She met an older man who worked on the docks, and he also took advantage of her and treated her horribly. She stayed with him for a year and a half until she couldn't stand the verbal and physical abuse any longer, and now, she's here in Sugar Sands. She's about out of money."

Keisha spoke out. "Let's help her."

Courtney and Coco looked at her with curiosity, and Keisha said.

"Oh, I'm sorry. Coco, I got so caught up in your story that I thought it was real. Go on." Together, they all gave a small laugh.

Coco continued. "She went to the Dollar General and, again, lied about her age and was able to get a job stocking shelves with merchandise during the graveyard shift. Another young man worked the same hours as she did, and they got to know each other pretty well. His name was Jamie. Eventually, he asked her out, and they went to the Seafood Shack. It was a great first date, but as you would expect, Ophelia kept her guard up. She did not want to be used and abused again. Over time, the two became closer and closer, so much so that Jamie wanted to marry her, but he couldn't until he found out the most important thing about her. Did she know Jesus as her Savior and Lord? He would never marry anyone who was not a Christian because the Bible says it's wrong to do that. One night, during one of their breaks at work, he asked her.

"Ophelia, I really love you, and I want to experience the rest of my life with you. I hope you feel the same way."

"Oh, I do." She responded.

He took her hand and spoke. "I have to ask you the most important question I could ever ask." She just knew he was going to ask her to marry him. "Ask away, Jamie," she said excitedly. "Have you ever asked Jesus into your life? Do you know Him as your Savior and Lord?"

She looked at him as if he was an alien. She immediately released his grip from her hand and ran away. After catching up to her, Jamie asked why she did that. She told him her mom's story and how that left a sour taste in her mouth about the church and God. He understood but told her that she couldn't let human choices give him a distorted view of God. He even gave her an example. He said you couldn't blame the violin's sound just because someone didn't play it well. So, you can't blame God when people don't live correctly. For the first time in the last three years of her life, she realized that was exactly what she was doing. Blaming God for something He didn't do. She hugged Jamie, and she gave her life to Christ right there on the spot. He then said that he had the second most important question to ask her. Cautiously, she asked him what that might be. He knelt down, looked into her eyes, and asked her if she would marry him. She said no."

The two girls, intently listening, said in unison. "What?"

Coco laughed and said. "I'm just kidding. She said yes."

Keisha and Courtney grabbed pillows and started pummeling Coco over and over.

Coco gave out a huge yawn and said, "I think I'm gonna get ready for bed."

Courtney commented, "Me, too, but we first have to decide who's sleeping on the floor since we only have two twin beds. I say we play rock, paper, scissors."

Keisha offered. "I don't mind sleeping on the floor."

"No way, Keisha. We'll play two outta three to see who's the loser."

Coco said. "Okay. Let's do it, but it's only fair to tell you two that I rarely ever lose when I play this game." Keisha said with her game face on.

"We'll see," Courtney said. Ready?"

They all threw out their hands, and Courtney won the first game. Keisha won the second, and Coco won the third one.

"This is the tiebreaker. Here goes." Courtney said with confidence.

Coco won the fourth game. "Hey, wait. I've got a better idea. Why don't we put the mattresses next to each other on the floor? That way, we can all sleep together on the floor."

Both Keisha and Courtney thought the idea was perfect. The girls wore their pajamas, brushed their teeth, and jumped onto the mattresses. It was a little tight, but the girls loved it. After saying their prayers, they yelled downstairs that they were going to sleep. Both Courtney's parents hollered back up for them to sleep well. Then, the girls had a short prayer time and said goodnight to each other. They were looking forward to spending more time together tomorrow.

The ringing of his cell phone awakened Al from the pawn shop.

"Why in the devil's name are you calling me this late? It's after midnight."

"Shut up! I'll call you whenever. Now listen up. The other voice said. Your two punks here in Sugar Sands are getting sloppy. I got word that they broke into a condo yesterday of two teenage girls who they helped the day before with jellyfish stingers. The girls were inside at the same time."

Al asked the caller. "Did the girls see them?"

"No, but the girls figured out it was them because they said they heard the men say something about the smell of Aloe Vera and Vinegar that they told them to use on their legs. Those same girls saw the knuckleheads in their truck earlier today at the Dollar General after they almost ran over them. These guys really must be idiots. I've been working too long and hard on this situation for it to go down the toilet just because of a couple of stupid punks. So, help me, Al, if you don't straighten them out, I will. And you better make sure your other knucklehead employees aren't being careless. I don't have to tell you that it only takes two or three idiots to mess up everything. I've built up my network to six pawnshops. It's been a perfect money-maker so far. Don't screw it up by using stupid people. If you can't handle being my manager, I'll find someone who can."

"Yeah, okay, boss. I get it. I'll talk to them tomorrow."

"Tell them another screwup, and they're dead."

Al wasn't sure if the other voice meant dead or just out of the deal. Either way, he would call them tomorrow.

"One more mess up, and you're both out. Do you understand?" Al demanded.

Steve responded. "Yeah, okay, but how could we have known those brats were in the condo? Before going in, we yelled out if anyone was there."

Al answered. "I don't care what you did, just don't screw up again and get me some more stock for my store, quick."

"Okay, Al." Steve turned his cell off and called Al some very unpleasant names.

Robbie asked him what was wrong.

"Don't worry about it. We gotta get some more merchandise, and my genius idea I've come up with might do the trick."

Robbie leaned in to hear what he had to say. He and Steve grew up in Pensacola and had been buddies for about three years. Really, rather than buddies, they were partners in crime. They had done everything from home break-ins to store robberies and made most of their money by hocking what they stole with a guy in Pensacola, Florida, who owned six pawn shops. He didn't always give them the best deal, but it was a way to get rid of the stolen merchandise and cash in on the stolen merchandise. Also, if they were ever suspected of anything, they didn't have the items to implicate or incriminate themselves.

Steve continued with his idea. "We go back to the beach and find some unsuspecting old people. It doesn't matter if they're a couple or single. We walk to where they might be sitting and strike up a conversation with them."

"About what?" Robbie inquired.

"Leave that to me. I've got plenty of ideas of what to talk to them about. The whole idea is to win their trust and confidence in us."

"I don't get it, Steve."

"Look, let's say we find an older couple sitting together on the beach. I sit a few feet from them, and after a while, I strike up a discussion about me and my brother."

"Your brother? I didn't think you had a brother."

"You're an idiot! I'm pretending with them about my so-called brother. I'll tell them that he's fallen on some troubled times. His wife and kids just left him because he lost the construction job he was working at. Now he's completely broke. I'll tell them that I've helped him as much as I could, but I'm tapped out, too. That's when you walk over to us, and I introduce you to them as my brother. You say hi, and then you turn to me and say that the convenience store wasn't hiring."

Robbie took off his ballcap and scratched his head. "What convenience store?"

Steve put his head back down and shook it back and forth. "It's not a real store, idiot. It's one that you say you went to hoping to find a job."

"Oh, I get it. You're trying to get them to feel sorry for us and give us a job."

"Really, Robbie? Are you that stupid? We're not going to work for them or anyone else. Hopefully, they'll offer to give us some money."

"What if that doesn't work, Steve?"

Steve answered, "I'll think of something else."

Keisha woke up first and noticed Courtney was sleeping on the floor. Coco was sound asleep next to her on the mattress. She got up, went out on the balcony with her phone, and pulled up the You version app. It was a terrific app for reading the Bible. Coco opened her eyes, stretched, and then joined Keisha.

"Hey, Keisha. Sleep, okay?"

"Yeah. Surprisingly good. How 'bout you?"

"Okay. Every now and then, Courtney would accidentally elbow me in the ribs in her sleep, which woke me up. I noticed she must have slid off onto the floor in the middle of the night."

"Yeah, I saw that. Hope she slept okay."

"She could sleep through a tornado. What 'cha reading?"

"One of my favorite Psalms. Chapter 23."

"Our Sunday morning Bible teacher challenged our class to memorize that chapter. It's been a while, but let me see if I remember it." Coco asked.

"Go for it." Keisha challenged.

Coco began, and Keisha had to give some assistance only a couple of times. Coco said after the struggle.

"I need to brush up on that, for sure."

Coco saw Courtney walking toward them. "Well, hey, sleepy head. Me and Keisha have been out here reading the Bible for about three hours."

"Oh, super spiritual girls, huh? Well, I got up about three hours before that and read through Galatians, Ephesians, and Colossians, then studied the book of Revelation."

They all burst into laughter. Keisha made a nose-smelling motion.

"Something smells amazing."

The girls decided to go downstairs and check it out.

Vicki and Melinda had made pancakes, waffles, bacon, and sausage.

"Oh, great. Why can't we ever eat without being bothered by teenage hoodlums?" Tim joked.

"No kidding, Tim. I thought they'd be in jail by now." Ralph quipped back.

Tim asked them what their plans were today.

Coco responded, "We thought about breaking into a couple of banks."

Courtney jumped into the fictitious narrative and added.

"Then we discussed flying to Paris to steal some high-end jewelry."

Then Keisha added. "And then we thought we'd steal a huge yacht and sell around the world."

Ralph replied, "Keisha, we hoped that you would be a good influence on these two, but we can see they have taken you down the dark road of destruction they are traveling."

Of course, everyone gave out a big chuckle about all their silliness.

"Would it be okay to just hang out at the beach?" Courtney asked.

"Yeah, Coco added, maybe do some walking toward the Hangout, too."

The adults looked at each other in agreement that their plans would be fine as long as they were careful. Vicki asked Keisha.

"Keisha, make sure you call your parents and see if that's okay with them."

"Yes, ma'am."

"Coco asked, "What are y'all doing today?"

Tim answered. "Me and Ralph have that appointment later with his celebrity idol, the Bama Beach Bum. Keisha's dad is going to join us, too."

Melinda said. "Keisha's mom and me and Vicki are going to the outlet stores this morning."

"Well, you adults, be sure and be careful." Courtney jokingly said.

The adults rolled their eyes at her, and, of course, Melinda fluttered her eyelids as only she could do.

After helping clear the table, the girls went upstairs to prepare for a fabulous day.

Vicki yelled up to them, "Don't forget to put on some sunscreen."

The girls shouted back that they would. After smearing on the lotion, they put their bathing suits, shorts, and a shirt over them and slipped on their sandals.

"I've got an idea that might be fun. What do you two say we have a scavenger hunt challenge?" Coco asked.

"Hmm, that sounds pretty fun. Courtney answered. What do you think, Keisha.?"

"I'm game. How does it work?"

Coco responded. "We'll write out a list of ten items that we want to look for. Each item will have points attributed to them. For instance, a comb might be worth thirty-five points. A pencil would be worth ten."

"Cool. What's the prize gonna be for the winner?" Keisha asked.

Courtney answered. "We've only played for fun, but I like the idea of ramping up the competition. What do you two think of this? The one who wins gets to fix the loser's hair any way she wants, and they have to wear it that way all the next day?"

They laughed together, then Keisha added. "Also, they have to wear two different types of shoes."

They all laughed again. Coco gave her two cents. "And the loser has to serve us our plates at dinner tonight."

They agreed on all the craziness, got three lists of the items they would scavenge for, and then awarded each one of the items listed. They couldn't wait to get the day started.

They ran downstairs, and Coco asked her mom if they could have three plastic bags. She found some that they had gotten when they went shopping. Each girl grabbed one and told them that they would see them later.

Ralph said, "Well, I was going to give you three some money to eat lunch, but since you're in such a hurry…"

The girls came back in, and he shucked out $10 for each one. They told him thanks, and they were off again. Melinda shouted as they were halfway out the door.

"And.."

Before she could finish her sentence, the girls said in unison, "We know! Be careful."

The girls ran down to the shoreline; the water was a perfect temperature. The sky was a blue that only God could color, and the sun was sparkling off of the sugar-white sand. They put their scavenger bags down with their towels, took off their sandals and outer garments they had over their bathing suits, and played in the small tide coming in and out. After an hour of body surfing and dunking each other, they decided to walk up toward the Hangout area. They toweled off, put their shorts, shirts, and sandals on, seized their bags, and headed that way. The scavenger hunt was on. They found things like a Zero Coke can, a hairbrush, a scarf, and various other articles they had written down. The points were quickly adding up. Every now and then, you would hear one of the girls squeal with excitement that they had found another item. You would have thought they were playing for $1000.00.

They were getting hungry, so they stopped at a small taco stand that was on the beach, where Coco ordered a meat and bean burrito with sour cream. Courtney got a soft taco with just meat and cheese. Keisha got an enchilada, and they all also split some loaded nachos.

"Boy, this was good, but I'm full as a tick," Courtney said.

Keisha replied. "Gross!

They all giggled as Coco let out a big burp after her big sip of Mountain Dew. All of a sudden, Coco stopped and discreetly pointed in the direction of the nearby pier. They looked at Coco and where she was pointing with curiosity.

"Slide over here and get behind this sign with me," Coco said.

The sign was in the sand on the left side advertising Hugo's Taco Stand.

"What's going on, Coco?" Courtney asked.

"Over there at the entrance of the pier. It's them, the so-called pre-med students."

Courtney and Keisha glanced that way.

Courtney responded, "You're right, Coco. Let's call our dads and tell them."

Courtney tried her cell, but her signal was too weak. Coco tried hers. Same thing. They gave Keisha Tim's number, and her signal, too, was not allowing the call to go through. "Unbelievable!" Coco exclaimed.

"Hey, let's get closer so we can watch where they go. Follow me." Courtney said.

Keisha and Coco slowly proceeded behind Courtney. They were able to find cover behind a beach tent and two chairs that weren't being used. It was fifty feet or so away from the pier. "So, these are the two guys supposedly stealing things from the condos?" Keisha asked quietly.

"Yeah. Coco answered. I wonder what they're doing."

The girls watched as the two young men stood at the pier entrance and did some people-watching. Occasionally, they tried unsuccessfully to talk to girls who would walk by them.

"Well, Steve. That was a great idea you had. We made a total of thirty bucks." Robbie said with frustration.

"Shut up, Robbie. It's thirty bucks we didn't have. You haven't had any smart ideas since you were three years old." Steve responded.

He was looking around, and Robbie asked what he was looking for. After a few minutes, Steve said, "I got it. Follow me."

They walked down the shoreline. The three girls followed and were careful not to be detected. Robbie noticed Steve looking at the different condo buildings.

When Steve stopped, Robbie asked, "What are you looking at, Steve?"

"For the right situation that fits into my plan. Go get our truck from the grocery store where we parked it and bring it as close as possible to the front of that condo."

As Steve pointed at the twelve-story condo, Robbie did as he was told. Steve went straight to a storage bin, where he noticed an employee going back and forth, putting away assorted items that had been rented. He had just locked up the bin and left. Steve jimmied the padlock with his special tool and was able to get it unlocked. After Robbie parked the truck, he walked to where Steve was.

Steve grabbed Robbie's shoulder and said, "Listen. If anyone asks what we're doing, we tell 'em we're employees and moving some items to another location. Got it?"

"Yeah. I ain't dumb." Robbie answered.

"That's up for debate," Steve replied.

Robbie looked at him with a question on his face.

They grabbed ten umbrellas and placed them into the bed of Steve's truck. They went back to the bin, snatched fourteen folding beach chairs, and put them into the bed. They returned one more time, took six carrying cases with volleyballs and nets in them, and threw them into the back of the truck, too.

"Jump in, Robbie. We need to get outta here before someone catches on that we aren't really employees."

Steve drove across the street to the same grocery store where his truck was parked earlier. They pulled a large grey tarpaulin over the stash to make sure it wouldn't be seen.

"That was a great idea, Steve. I never would have thought about grabbing all that stuff. Al will love it."

"That's why I'm the brains, Robbie."

Robbie just shook his head in agreement. Steve had some more plans before they went to Pensacola and cashed in on their recently stolen items.

They exited the van, and Steve said to Robbie, "Let's go back to the pier."

The girls watched the so-called pre-med students the whole time from behind a small wooden fence. After watching them put the items into their truck, they saw them heading back toward the pier.

"Duck down, y'all. Coco said. We can't let them see us."

It was too late. Steve had already seen them. The young men walked toward them and stopped at the fence.

Steve commented, "Well, if it's not the girls we helped the other day. You two must be feeling better, and what are you doing way down this way, sitting by this fence? You're quite a long way from your condo."

"Yeah, I remember where it is because we came by to see." Steve shut Robbie up quickly before he said anything stupid.

Steve continued. "You girls wouldn't be following us around, now, would you? And who's your little friend?"

The girls remained quiet and didn't answer.

"Cat must have your tongues." Steve knelt down, got close to their faces, and said, "Let's make sure we don't see you again. Hear? Now git!"

The girls stood up and ran in the other direction toward the taco stand. When they got out of view, they hid behind another sign on the beach and watched what the creeps' next move would be.

"I'm getting a little scared, y'all," Keisha commented nervously.

"We are, too, Keisha, but we gotta see what else they might do so we can tell the police." Coco replied.

They observed Steve and Robbie walking back toward the same condo they were in earlier. They rinsed the sand off their feet in the pool's shower and put their sandals back on. "Come on." Courtney encouraged. "Let's go up here and get behind the tall fence that separates the condos."

It took them about a minute to run there, but they were well hidden, and they spotted the men standing in the parking lot in front of the condo beside a black SUV. Finally, they walked away from the SUV and headed up the stairwell.

"I wonder where they're going now?" Keisha questioned.

"It looks like they're going up the stairwell," Coco replied.

The girls couldn't see them once they were in the stairwell, but eventually, they stepped out on the eighth floor and went directly to one of the rooms on the eighth floor.

"Didn't a family just leave that room?" Coco asked the girls.

Courtney answered, "I believe I saw them headed to the beach."

Steve appeared to be working on getting the door open, while Robbie seemed to be on the lookout.

"We need to recheck our phones to see if there's a better signal," Coco said.

They did, and still, they each had only one bar.

"Hey, they got in," Courtney said with desperation, pointing toward the room. What do we do?"

"Let's just keep our eyes peeled on the room and see what happens next. Who knows? Maybe this is where they're staying with their family or some friends." Coco responded.

"I doubt it, Coco," Courtney said with a sly look.

The three girls stood there for quite a few minutes; then they spotted the two men coming out. It appeared that one had a pillowcase stuffed with some items and was carrying a vacuum cleaner, and the other was carrying a flat TV. They saw them disappear into the stairwell and walk through the parking lot and across the street to the grocery store, where they loaded their bounty.

"Man, we missed catching them again. They've gotta get caught." Courtney said with irritation.

"Seriously! Well, there's nothing we can do now. Let's get back to the condo and tell our parents." Coco replied.

Keisha added, "We should get the room number they were in so the police can visit the family and tell them what happened."

Both Courtneys answered that that was a great idea.

They jetted back to the condo as fast as their legs would go. They rushed into the bottom floor sliding glass door and almost hit Cindy.

Melinda said, "Whoa, ladies. You three going to a fire?"

Courtney blared out. "Mom, we saw them again."

"Saw who, honey?"

Coco jumped in. "The pre-med students."

"What! Where and when did you see them?" Vicki anxiously asked.

Courtney took her turn again and answered them. "We were playing our scavenger game, and we noticed them at the front entrance of the pier near the Hangout."

All three girls continued adding bits and pieces of information to the whole story.

"Did they see you?" Vicki asked.

"At first, they didn't. We were cautious not to let them see us following them." Coco answered.

Courtney interjected. "But they saw us hiding behind the small fence when they walked back to the pier. They warned us to stop following them and they better not see us again."

Melinda added. "You three following them wasn't the wisest thing to do in the first place."

"Yeah, but mom, Courtney returned. We wouldn't have seen where they were going and what they were doing if we hadn't."

Melinda and the other ladies revealed displeasure on their faces yet appreciated the girl's fearlessness in gathering this vital information about the so-called pre-med student's criminal activities.

At that moment, Ralph, Tim, and Silas walked in, and Ralph said. "Well, lookie, lookie here."

As he held up his fishing rod signed by the Bama Beach Bum, all the females looked at him, and Silas commented. "He'll never use that rod again!"

He and Tim laughed. The men noticed that the others weren't interested, nor did they join in the laughter.

Tim commented, "Why the gloomy looks, ladies? Y'all look like you've been to a funeral?"

Vicki responded. "Sorry, Ralph, that we can't share in your excitement at the moment, but the girls just told us that while they were out, they stumbled upon the two young men the police are looking for."

Ralph asked. "What happened, girls?"

Again, all three girls told the narrative with as much information as they could remember.

Tim said with much concern. "Why didn't you girls call us? I can appreciate the detective work, but you should have called us. This is not a game."

Vicki chimed in and told Tim that they tried but didn't have good cell service.

"Don't you think we should call the police and inform them?" Silas asked.

"Absolutely," Tim replied.

He dialed the station and asked for Officer Watson or Chief Graham. He was put on hold for a few seconds, and then the desk Officer came back on the line. He told Tim neither of them was in, and he could get the info and pass it on. Tim proceeded to give him all the details the girls had given them. He sounded extremely appreciative and said he'd follow up on the information.

Then Tim looked at the girls and calmly said. "Ladies, understand. We're not angry with you three, but from now on, please don't do anything like this again. We don't know how dangerous these two men could be."

The girls nodded in agreement.

After the initial excitement of the day started wearing off, all three families enjoyed spending the afternoon together. The adults drank coffee and ate some leftover doughnuts while the girls went upstairs and goofed off with a couple of board games.

Melinda called upstairs and said to the girls. "Ladies, the Bradford's are eating with us tonight, and we're gonna grill out hotdogs and burgers tonight. We'll be eating in about an hour."

The girls were super excited about those plans. While waiting for dinner, they decided to go outside and throw the frisbee.

As the so-called pre-med students were driving to the Pensacola pawn shop, Robbie asked. "What do you think Al is gonna give us for all the stuff we got today, Steve?"

"I don't know, but it better be more than what he's been giving us." Steve answered.

They walked inside right at closing time. Al was about to lock the front door. He let them in and spoke.

"I was just about to leave. This better be worth staying for. If your stuff ain't any better than the lame stuff you've been bringing lately, I might have to improve my employee situation. What cha got?"

They went back outside and brought it all into his store. After Al saw all the items, he looked at Steve and Robbie with much approval.

"Now, this is more like it. I knew you two bozos had it in you. This jewelry isn't worth nothin', but this other stuff is the merch I can sell."

Al went to the other side of the counter and began writing out a check for them.

"You're gettin' $400.00 for all of it. Pretty good haul, you two. Keep this up, and you'll make some money. Remember, big, ticketed items. I'm also looking for house and lawn equipment like pressure washers, leaf blowers, edgers, and power tools. Capisci?"

"Huh?" Robbie asked.

Steve slapped him across the back of his head and told him that meant "understand."

"Oh, I didn't know you could speak a foreign language, Al."

Al just rolled his eyes and shook his head.

Steve spoke. "Thanks, boss. We'll keep at it."

"Yeah, yeah, now get outta here. I got a 16 ounce ribeye waiting on me at home."

Al stopped them before they made it out of the front door.

"And don't get sloppy. You get careless, and you get caught. We don't want it to happen, or there might be some serious consequences for you two. I'll say it again. Capisci?"

The young men nodded that they understood, got in the truck, went through Checkers drive-thru, and got some burgers, fries, and a drink to eat on their way back to Sugar Sands. They pulled into the vacant condo's driveway off the beaten path. It was just one of the most recent condos that Steve and Robbie had broken into. They parked behind it so that the truck wouldn't be as noticeable. After they got inside, they laid down on blankets and a couple of pillows they'd taken from one of the condos a few weeks earlier.

"Robbie, we did pretty good this time. I gotta think of more ideas so we can continue building our enterprise."

Robbie agreed.

CHAPTER FIVE: GETTING SLOPPY

The grilled burgers and hotdogs hit the spot, but the pecan pie and ice cream really put it over the top. Everyone helped to put the food away and clean the dishes. The adults sat around the dinner table discussing their day. The guys talked about their fishing experience with the Bama Beach Bum while the women spoke about their shopping excursion. The girls were in the den sitting on the floor, talking about the excitement of their day.

Coco yelled out, "Wait a minute. We never added up the items we found. We don't know who won the scavenger hunt."

Courtney answered. "Yeah, with all the excitement, we forgot all about it."

"Let's go upstairs and get our bags, but really, there's probably no use because I know it's gonna be me who won." Keisha bragged jokingly.

The other two girls gave her a skeptical look. The girls ran upstairs, grabbed their bags, and came back downstairs to count the items to see who won the hunt.

Keisha yelled out, "I've got mine counted. 350 points."

Surprised, Courtney said, "No way! That's what I have."

Coco added. "What! You two have exactly what I have. What are the chances of that happening."

That was too uncanny. They giggled and chuckled until their stomachs ached.

Once Coco gathered her composure, she said. "And I was looking forward to fixing y'all's hair the silliest way I could think of."

"Me, too." Keisha added.

"Well, not me. In fact, if I had won, I wasn't going to do anything to either of you." Courtney said with a smug and fake self-righteousness look.

"Yeah, right." Keisha and Coco said in unison while grabbing a couple of couch cushions and pummeling her with them.

Cindy and Silas thanked the Sims and Lawrences for supper, invited them to join them for the day, and then excused themselves to return to their condo.

"Let's go, spunky."

Both Courtneys looked at Keisha and said in unison. "Spunky!"

"Yeah, yeah, yeah. That's what Dad has called me since I was three or four."

"Yep. Silas interjected. She was always so full of energy and getting into everything she could get her hands on. That's when I started calling her that. She'll always be my little Spunky."

 Keisha turned a little red, but you could tell it was a term of endearment that she really enjoyed. She loved her dad and mom very much but knew she was her daddy's girl.

"Can Keisha stay another night with us?" Coco asked the Bradfords.

Before they could answer, Ralph said it would be fine with them if they didn't care.

Silas answered. "I guess so, as long as the Sims and Lawrences aren't tired of you yet. It just gives me and your mom more honeymooning time."

Keisha said, "Dad. Gross!"

Tim, Ralph, Vicki, and Melinda got a rise out of Silas' remark and chuckled.

Cindy looked at Silas, grabbed him, and spoke. "Let's go before you get yourself into trouble."

"By the way, Ralph, Keisha told me you spotted her a ten to eat on today. Thanks for doing that. Here."

Silas handed Ralph a ten-dollar bill.

"That's not necessary, Silas."

"No, take it. We probably owe you a whole lot more for putting up with our daughter." Silas kidded.

"Yeah. Keisha has been a whole lot of trouble." Melinda kidded back.

They all laughed and said their goodbyes. The girls went upstairs and got ready for bed. After brushing their teeth and sharing a devotion together, they got into their floor bed and watched the Netflix movie, "Mary Magdalene." It was about one of the few women who were a part of Jesus of Nazareth's following. She defied societal norms and family expectations to experience a true spiritual awakening. They all fell asleep before it was over, and later that night, Coco woke up, turned off the TV, and then jumped back onto the mattresses.

"That's it, Al. Get rid of them, or I will."

"What happened?" Al inquired of his boss, who was steaming on the other end.

"Those teenage girls must have recognized them and followed them. They saw them steal some beach supplies and break into a room at one of the condos. They were able to give all kinds of details to the police. I told you, these guys are idiots. I'm throwing you under the bus if they get caught and talk. I ain't going down. You understand?"

"Okay. Okay. I'll call 'em and tell them they're out. I know a couple of other chumps I can get to do this."

"Now, Al! Get rid of them now!" the other voice on the other end demanded.

Al immediately called Steve.

Steve answered his cell. "Yessir. What's up?"

"My boss just told me that those two teenage girls you helped the other day saw you breaking into the condo where you got the TV and vacuum. And they saw you bozos grabbing the beach merchandise. This is what I meant when I said you can't get sloppy."

Steve interrupted Al.

"Sorry, boss. "Yeah, well, sorry, doesn't get it. I'm supposed to get rid of you two."

Steve begged, "Come on, boss. Give us another chance. We'll do better and be more careful, I promise."

"Well, this last haul you two made was much better. I guess I'll give you one more opportunity. I want to see some high-end merchandise here by the middle of next week. You hear?"

"Yessir, boss. Thanks, boss. You'll be glad you made this decision. I promise."

"Yeah, yeah, yeah." See you next week. Don't make any more problems!"

"Those punk kids have really caused us problems. We gotta do something about them." Steve angrily said.

Robbie just stared at Steve, not knowing what to say, but he didn't like his last statement, that was for sure. He didn't want any kids getting hurt.

CHAPTER SIX: WATERVILLE SCARE

"The week has gone by way too fast. It's already Friday, and we're leaving tomorrow." Courtney said, waking up the other two girls.

"Thanks for waking us up, Court," Coco said while pulling her pillow over her head.

"Well, it's already 10:00 a.m., and we only have today left. We gotta get up and see what trouble we can get into."

"10:00? I didn't realize it was that late." Coco replied.

"Excuse me, but someone is trying to get some sleep over here." Keisha jokingly said.

Courtney looked at Keisha and teased. "Get up, Spunky. It's 10:00, and we gotta have some extreme fun since it's our last day."

Keisha squinted at Courtney and said, "What's the plan?"

Coco answered, "Haven't gotten any yet. What do y'all want to do?"

They all thought for a moment, and then Courtney suggested they get dressed, eat breakfast, and then figure out what they would do. All agreed and did just that. The adults had already eaten and told the sleepy heads that there were sausage biscuits in the oven.

"About time you three got outta bed. We thought you were just going to sleep all day." Ralph said.

"Well, Ralph, they do need their beauty sleep. In fact, Ralph, when does beauty sleep start to take effect?"

"I don't know, Tim, but hopefully, it will start soon with these three."

They both laughed at their kidding them.

Melinda chimed in. "You two could sleep for a hundred more years, and it wouldn't help your looks."

Ralph answered. "That really hurts, honey. You know you married me for my looks."

"Well, it sure wasn't for your money." She spurted back.

Everyone chuckled.

"What are your plans today, girls?" Vicki asked.

Coco replied, "Not sure yet, Mom. We're still trying to come up with something."

"So, no bank robbing, jet airliner stealing, or yacht theft today, huh?" Vicki teased.

All three smiled at the comment.

Tim offered an idea. "What would you think about going to Waterville this afternoon?"

Coco replied, "Seriously? That sounds great."

The other two girls complied.

"Vic, Mel, what do y'all think?"

"That'll be fine if you all want to go, but I think I want to just relax today around the pool and maybe even out on the beach." Melinda replied.

"Now that sounds great, Melinda. Vicki commented. I think I'll join you. In fact, why don't we call Cindy and see if she wants to join us if they haven't already got some other plans? Silas probably would enjoy going to Waterville with you all."

"Yeah. Give her a call, Vic." Melinda answered.

Vicki called, and the plans were made. Silas would drop Cindy off at the condo and join Tim, Ralph, and the girls at Waterville. Cindy said they'd be there around noon, allowing everyone to grab a bite.

The dads bought a day's ticket for each of their daughters and let the girls do whatever they wanted to. They decided leaving their cellphones in a rented locker would be best because they might get lost or wet during the rides. They planned to check in at the go-carts at the top of every hour to ensure all was well.

"Come on, Coco yelled, let's go over to the Cannonball Run."

Keisha and Courtney joined her, and that started an incredible day of fun. The dads even rode with them on a couple of rides. Tim got called by one of the workers at the go-carts to slow down and quit bumping into the other carts. He told the worker that that guy started it while pointing to Ralph. Ralph laughed. The girls tried the Flowrider, but it was much more difficult than it looked. The line to do it again was extraordinarily long, so they decided to go to Wa-Wa World and hit the wave pool. Time was flying by, and they hadn't ever gone to the lazy river yet, so that's where they headed. Each one grabbed an innertube, sat down in the river, and enjoyed a relaxing float until they heard someone next to them.

"Well, look, who's here? Good to see you girls again. You two seem to be popping up wherever we are."

Seeing Steve and Robbie caught the three girls off guard so much that they didn't say anything.

Courtney finally gathered some strength and said to the men. "You better get away from us, or we'll scream."

There were only a few exits out of the lazy river, so they couldn't escape them yet.

"Screaming wouldn't be your best alternative. We're exceptionally good at making accidents fatal. I mean, you two could drown in this little river very easily."

They finally got to one of the exits and started getting out of their innertubes, but Steve grabbed Coco, and Robbie took Steve's lead and grabbed Courtney, and they pushed them back down. Keisha jumped out and ran as fast as she could to find her dad, Tim, and Ralph.

Steve told Robbie not to worry about her.

He looked back at the Courtneys. "Don't be so quick to leave our company, girls."

Courtney and Coco looked terrified at each other.

"What are you gonna do to us?" Courtney asked.

Steve responded. "Who said we were going to do anything to you? We just wanna have a quick little conversation with you two. Now, here comes another one of the exits, and we four are going to step out just like we're a sweet little family. Again, I would encourage you two to comply, or there's a possibility you just might incur an accident."

Keisha was frantically running throughout the water park. She wasn't having any fortune finding either of the dads. She noticed that it was a couple of minutes to the top of the hour, so she decided the best thing to do would be to wait at the go-carts area until the dads arrived.

The two so-called pre-med students, Courtney and Coco, stepped out of the lazy river exit. Steve pulled Coco, and Robbie pulled Courtney by their arms. They did their best to keep curious onlookers from noticing anything strange and peculiar as the men walked them toward the parking lot.

"Where are you taking us?" Coco asked desperately.

"Shut up and don't make any needless noises or unnecessary motions that might get people's attention, and you two will end up fine. Understand?"

The Courtneys barely nodded.

Tim and Ralph saw Keisha at the go-carts area and were about to ask where the Courtneys were when Keisha loudly said.

"The guys took them."

Her dad said, "What? You mean the two guys who's been breaking into the condos?"

"Yessir."

"Where did they take them, Keisha?" Tim asked.

"I don't know. We were in the lazy river, and that's where they grabbed them. I was able to get away and waited here to find you."

"Look! In the parking lot." Ralph had spotted the two men attempting to force their girls into their truck.

All of them ran toward the parking lot and yelled at them to stop. Tim remembered, turned around, and went to the locker where they had stashed their cell phones. The men saw Ralph and Silas coming toward them. They released their grip on the girls, threw them down, jumped in their truck, and drove away.

Ralph said to the girls, Silas and Tim. "Come on. Get into the car."

They did and began chasing the Tacoma, which turned left and headed north on Highway 59. Tim dialed the police station to tell them about the recent situation.

"I need to speak to Chief Graham now, and please hurry up."

The desk Officer asked what the call was about. Tim tried his best to tell the desk Officer without sounding mean or demanding, but he really didn't have time to go over the details with him. The Officer told Tim they should not follow them because they could be armed and dangerous. Tim told him they would take their chances and just get him to Chief Graham on the phone. Finally, the Officer complied with the request.

Ralph was following the young men as closely as he could. They were about a mile behind them, trying their best to keep up. The heavy traffic wasn't helping. The desk Officer came back on the line.

"Chief Graham isn't here. He's out on a call. Just give me the details, and I'll dispatch it to him."

"What about Officer Watson?" Tim asked.

"He's not here either. Just tell me what's going on."

"We are currently in our vehicle chasing two men who have been breaking into the condos."

"Yeah, I know about them. Look, sir. You don't need to be this involved. It's difficult to drive on Highway 59 in normal circumstances, but it's even more life-threatening when you're trying to chase someone. You don't want to cause any accidents. And what if you do catch up to them, and they're armed, and they start shooting at you? All kinds of scenarios could put you and the others in your vehicle at risk and in a very harmful and precarious situation. Tell me where you are exactly, and I'll put out an APB on the Tacoma."

Tim gave him their location and told the Officer they would continue in pursuit until they saw police intervention.

"What didn't you understand about getting rid of those punks?"

Al, surprised by the call, answered with a lie. "I did. I told them they were out. They argued a little and tried to talk me into giving them another chance, but I told them no way. What happened?"

"Those punk kids and their dads saw them at Waterville and called the police station. If those idiots get caught and talk, I swear, AL. Call 'em now and tell them to get out of Sugar Sands and tell them if they don't, I'll make sure they leave in a body bag."

"Yeah, okay. I'll call 'em right now."

Al wiped the sweat off his brow and called the two young men.

Steve answered his cell and asked, "Yeah."

"What have you idiots done now? The boss just called me and said you two made another mess that's gonna have to be cleaned up."

"We saw those two girls at the water park and were going to just scare them to keep them quiet. Their dads saw us, so we got in the truck and sped out of the parking lot. They were chasing us, but we think we lost them."

"You two keep driving straight up Highway 59 and don't stop. Your lives are in serious danger if you don't. My boss told me if you two are seen even close to Sugar Sands, he'll make sure you leave in two body bags. Get outta town now! I don't want to hear from you again."

Al threw his cell phone onto a couch in his office.

They just couldn't keep up with Tacoma with all the crazy traffic and didn't want to endanger themselves and other commuters on the road.

Tim, Ralph, Silas, and their girls walked into the Sims and Lawrence's condo, and frustration showed all over their faces.

Melinda asked. "Oh no. What now?"

They entered into the recent narrative and told the ladies everything that had happened. Tim decided to call for Chief Graham again. He hoped the desk Officer had contacted him about their recent encounter with the two perps. The voice that answered was different this time.

"Sugar Sands Police Station, how can I help you?"

"Yes, sir. This is Tim Lawrence, and I needed to speak to Chief Graham. Would he be in?"

"Let me check."

Shortly, Chief Graham was on the line.

"Chief Graham. How may I help you?"

"Hello, Chief. This is Tim Lawrence. Did the desk Officer from this morning tell you I had called?"

"I haven't been informed of any call from you, Mr. Lawrence. What were you calling about?"

Tim repeated the entire story to the Chief.

"Unbelievable! I haven't heard any of this. I'll get back to you. I've got some investigating I need to do."

They closed the call, and Tim told everyone about it.

The rich aroma of Lasagna was almost ignored with the upsetting news, but Ralph asked if that was lasagna cooking. The ladies told them that Cindy had a special recipe and thought they'd give it a try.

"It'll be ready in about an hour. Despite the episode with those hoodlums, did y'all have fun at Waterville?" Cindy asked.

"It was awesome." The girls replied.

The next fifteen minutes were a conversation saturated with all the details of each ride and experience. The girls said they were going upstairs to get cleaned up for supper.

After they had left, Tim opened up and spoke. "Is it just me, or does it seem that the local police aren't all that interested in catching these guys? I mean, they've come when called and taken down the information we gave, but I don't know, you'd think in a small community like Sugar Sands, they would have already spotted the truck and apprehended these guys."

"I wasn't going to say anything, Tim, but I'd been feeling the same way. Nice guys, but just don't seem to be terribly involved in the situation." Ralph interjected.

Vicki spoke up. "Well, in their defense, it is summertime, and a lot of students are spending time here. I'm sure they're having to follow up on all kinds of craziness and even criminal activity."

Melinda got their attention and told them something she'd found online. *"There are two police departments in Sugar Sands, Alabama, serving a population of 11,360 people in an area of twenty-seven square miles. There is one police department per 5,679 people and one police department per thirteen square miles.* And if I read it correctly, they only have forty-five Officers in the department. So, here again, in their defense, that's a lot of people to serve and keep the peace."

"Yeah, you have a point, Melinda. Silas said, but still, you'd think someone in law enforcement would have seen them."

CHAPTER SEVEN: WHO TO BELIEVE

"Where are we going, Steve?" Robbie asked while they were traveling up Highway 59. Steve didn't answer.

"Steve! I asked where are we going. You ain't said nothin' since we left Sugar Sands. What's going on, and what did Al tell you? Are we going to do another job for him or what?"

Steve still didn't say anything.

"You deaf? Steve! Why ain't you answering me? Hey!"

Steve jerked the car into a convenience store's parking lot in Bay Minette and slammed on the brakes.

Robbie almost hit his head on the dash and yelled out. "What are you doing? You crazy or somethin'?"

Steve grabbed Robbie by his shirt collar. "We're in trouble. Big trouble. Al said those stupid punk girls had identified us, and now the cops are looking for us. We're done with Al and working in Sugar Sands, so we gotta find another gig. So, shut up and let me think."

Robbie couldn't let that go without asking Steve again what they would do.

Steve said in a quieter voice, "I don't know. Just let me think."

They all gathered at the table, asked the Lord to bless the food, and started tearing into the lasagna. It was some of the best they'd ever eaten. Vicki and Melinda made sure to get Cindy's recipe. After eating, the ladies sat in the den drinking some coffee while the men went out to the balcony and sat. The girls went upstairs and ate some leftover brownies and milk.

Tim opened up and said. "Let me ask you two a couple of questions. Would you agree that Chief Graham and Officer Watson have been upstanding and seemingly interested and responsive in receiving the details that we've given them?"

Both agreed.

"Would you agree that they, as far as we know, have followed up on our information?"

Again, they both nodded yes.

"Me, too. With that being the case, why haven't those punks been caught or, at least, been seen? I know it's a small police department, like Melinda was saying, but still. Sugar Sands isn't that big. Here's a couple of theories I have. Tell me what you think about them. One, the two so-called pre-med students are the kids of some rich parents and are being protected. Two, Graham and Watson, are involved with the men and their criminal activity. Three, Graham and Watson and the other Officers aren't being given all the information, and number three is the one I'm more inclined to believe what is going on."

"I think I know where you're going, Tim," Ralph interposed. "You think the info is not getting to Graham or Watson. So, if they're not receiving the information, how could they be pursuing the leads they haven't even heard about."

"Exactly!" Tim explained.

Silas joined in. "If this theory of yours is correct, Tim, then that means someone is conspiring with the young perpetrators. If it's not Watson or Graham, who could it be?"

Tim showed signs of exasperation on his face and said. "I have to believe it's one of the desk Officers. I never got the name of any of them because they would always answer the same way, 'Sugar Sands Police station, how can I help you?'"

At that moment, Tim saw a call coming through on his cell, put it on speaker mode, and answered.

"Hello."

"Mr. Lawrence, this is Chief Graham. I've been doing a little investigation on something. Other than the original call about your condo being broken into this past Tuesday, how many additional times have you called this week asking for me or Officer Watson?"

"We called the next day about our girls seeing them at a Dollar General store," Tim answered.

Ralph jumped in and added. "This is Ralph Sims, Chief. We also called Thursday about the girls seeing the men loading up a ton of beach equipment into their truck and seeing another condo break in."

Tim interjected. "When the desk Officer told us you nor Officer Watson was available, he asked us to give him the information, and he'd make sure it got to one of you."

"Hmm, interesting. That's three times and four issues. Any other calls where you or Mr. Sims tried to reach either of us?" Chief Graham inquired.

"Yessir. I called yesterday about a scary confrontation we had at the waterpark." Ralph continued telling the Chief the whole incident.

"That's four individual times you or Mr. Sims have called the station, and as far as I know, Officer Watson and I only received the first call. Something is definitely awry. I don't want to make any rash conclusions at this time, but it would appear that Watson and I have been intentionally kept out of the loop. Thank you for your time tonight. I'll be getting back to you as soon as I have more evidence if, in fact, what

I'm thinking is true. By the way, this is my cell phone number. I'd appreciate you calling me directly if any other situations happen."

Tim said they would.

Silas spoke up and said, "It has to be one of the desk Officers."

"I agree, Silas," Ralph commented.

They opened the sliding glass door, came inside from the balcony, and informed the ladies of the conversation with the Chief.

"This is incredible!" Vicki exclaimed.

"Really. I can't believe another Officer could be involved with those two thieves." Cindy stated.

"I know. You see it on TV in a police series or movie but not in real life." Melinda remarked.

"Well, we better get back to our condo and get some rest. We're heading out tomorrow, and we've got a lot of packing to do." Cindy said.

Vicki responded. "Yeah, us, too. The worst part of vacationing."

"No. The worst part is unpacking when you get home." Melinda quipped with a flutter of her eyelids.

The ladies all agreed with that statement.

"Spunky, come on. We need to head out." Silas yelled to Keisha so she could hear her upstairs.

Keisha came down with the Courtneys. Everyone hugged like they had been friends for years.

"It was so nice to meet you all. We pray you'll have a safe trip home." Tim offered.

"Y'all, too," Cindy remarked.

"Let's all try and stay in touch. Maybe we can get together again." Ralph added.

Silas replied. "Sounds like a great plan."

"What a wonderful family!" exclaimed Melinda.

All commented the same.

"Yeah, and Keisha was a blast," Coco added.

"Really!" Courtney consented.

Tim's cell rang at that same time, and he recognized the number. He placed it on speaker mode and answered.

"Hello, Chief."

"Hello, Mr. Lawrence. I apologize for calling so late, but as I told you earlier, I've been doing a thorough probing into this situation with the two men's criminal activity. I've been mostly concerned with the lack of communication. Officer Watson and I wanted to come by your condo and speak with you all."

Tim looked up at the other adults for their approval and then told the Chief that would be fine.

"Thank you. Would it be okay to drop by now?"

"Sure. We'll be here."

"I wonder what they want to talk to us about?" Melinda pondered out loud.

"Maybe they have some more information about the two young men," Vicki commented.

Within thirty minutes, there was a knock on the condo's front door. Ralph opened it up and invited the Chief inside.

"Would you like a cup of coffee, Chief?" Vicki asked.

"That would be great. Thank you. Again, I realize it's late, and you all probably wonder why I needed to see you. What I'm about to tell you is very confidential and cannot be told to anyone outside us."

Melinda looked at the girls and said, "Girls, why don't you two go upstairs?"

The Courtneys, in unison, moaned in disagreement.

"Actually, if you all don't mind, I'd like them to hear what I have to say and get their input, as well, since they have been so involved."

All the adults agreed that it would be fine. The girls looked at each other and smiled. Everyone settled into the den. Vicki handed Chief Graham his coffee, and then he proceeded to tell them their purpose for seeing them and the urgency of the meeting.

CHAPTER EIGHT: THE PLAN

"After the call with you earlier, I was quite disturbed, to say the least, to find out how Officer Watson and I have allegedly been left out on the ongoing investigation with these two young men who have been breaking and entering into condos. I met with Officer Watson and informed him of our conversation, and after our discussion, we've concluded there must be someone on the inside that is involved with these two thieves."

Tim interrupted and candidly mentioned. "This is interesting that you two would be telling us this. We have recently been thinking the same thing, and to be honest, we didn't say anything because we thought it could possibly be one of you."

Officer Watson remarked. "We understand, Mr. Lawrence. Anyone would have had the same idea."

"Do you have any suspects?" Ralph asked.

Officer Watson answered, "We have a couple of subjects, but we don't have enough evidence to make any accusations. That's actually what we came to talk to you about."

Chief Graham interjected. "We have a plan that we wanted to run by you. It's a little crazy, and Watson and I still aren't really sure about the idea. That's why we want your feedback, and we would definitely need your approval to move ahead."

Curiosity filled the room.

"You two are sounding very mysterious, Chief." Melinda offered.

"I'm sure we are, Ms. Sims. I apologize and don't mean to give you reason for worry. Let me explain. A few years ago, our family owned a yellow and black cat. It was extremely active and curious, and because of this, he would occasionally get into precarious and dangerous places. We discovered the only way to lure him out was to offer it food. That would entice him just enough that we could grab him and get him out of the predicament he had gotten himself into. Officer Watson and I believe we need to do something similar. The only difference is, we don't know which cat, if you will, is the one that needs to be lured out."

Vicki interrupted. "Sounds like you're setting a trap like my father did when I was about nine or ten. We had a problem with an opossum that would burrow itself under our house. It would bring its meals into the location under our house and leave behind the leftovers. When the leftovers started to rot, it would attract flies and create a horrible smell. Not to mention the horrendous odor its excrement would leave. Sorry to be so gross."

They all kind of chuckled. Vicki continued with her story. "Dad eventually built a cage and put marshmallows in it. Sometimes, he used cat food. Both attracted the varmint into the cage. Once he crawled in, the door would automatically shut, and my dad would take the opossum out to the woods a few miles away and release it."

"Ms. Lawrence, you're actually right on target. That's the plan."

Officer Watson interjected, "That's basically what we would like to do. We have devised a plan to catch these road rats."

Another round of chuckles sounded throughout the den.

Tim anxiously asked. "Tell us about your idea."

Chief Graham resumed their idea. "We would like for you to call the police station tomorrow and tell the desk Officer who you are and that you would like to speak to one of us, just like you've done on the previous calls. If the Officer says that we're unavailable, he'll most likely ask you to give him the information so he can dispatch it to the Officers on patrol. Tell him you saw the two men at Alvin's who broke into your condo earlier this week. Watson and I will be at the station when you call. If the desk Officer doesn't relay the call to one of us, then we'll have a fairly good idea that he's involved with the duo and has been withholding information and not communicating the calls to us."

"So, I'm guessing you and Watson will confront him once he hangs up," Ralph questioned.

"No, sir. It will be just the beginning of a real investigation, then. We don't want to give him any indication that we are on to him. We will go to the judge, tell him the situation, and ask if we can begin surveillance of the desk Officer. That way, we can put a tracker on his vehicle, record his personal cell phone, and basically watch his every move."

Tim commented. "It sounds as if you want to catch him possibly having some association with the men, is that right?"

Chief Graham responded. "Yessir. Well, will you all agree to assist us with the call?"

Everyone looked at each other and asked them what they thought. All agreed that the plan might work and it was worth a try.

"Ralph, if it's okay, I'll call you tomorrow morning and let you know when to call." Chief Graham asked.

"Absolutely," Ralph said.

"Well, I'm going to bed since we've got to get up early tomorrow," Ralph said.

Everyone else agreed and went to their rooms.

"Hey, y'all, before we go, why don't we pray for Chief Graham and Officer Watson.?" Tim offered.

"Great idea." Melinda and Vicki said in unison.

Tim asked Ralph if he would pray.

"Be glad to."

They all held hands, and Ralph prayed.

"Father, we come to You asking that You give Chief Graham and Officer Watson the wisdom to handle this difficult situation. We pray that those involved with this illicit activity will get caught and brought to justice. Please protect them throughout this ordeal. Thank You, Lord, and we give You all the praise and glory. In Jesus's precious name, amen."

All said amen and headed to their rooms for the night.

"Why are you turning around, Steve? I thought Al told us to get away from Sugar Sands." Robbie asked.

"No one tells me what to do. I'm sick and tired of being the smuck. I'm gonna start making my own plans and make some real money."

"Yeah, okay, but what's your plan? Don't we need to be careful that the police don't catch us in Sugar Sands?" Robbie inquired.

Steve answered, "They ain't gonna catch us. Don't you get it, numbskull? According to Al, there have been a couple of calls from that family that have those stupid girls. The police should have already found us and taken us in. I mean, come on. We've been out in the open this whole time. We've even seen some local cops pass us and never blink an eye."

Robbie paused for a moment, thought, and then remarked. "I ain't never thought about that. That is kinda weird."

"No, it ain't weird, nitwit. Whoever has been calling, Al must be working for the police and pulling all the strings. Whoever it is must be Al's boss. Get it, bozo?"

"You ain't gotta keep callin' me names, Steve."

"Shut up and listen up, Robbie. You're gonna have to make a choice because I'm gonna make some changes, and it's gonna start with those two bratty girls. They've messed everything up for us, and it's gonna stop."

Robbie was confused by what Steve was inferring asked.

"What are you thinking about doing?"

"I'm not sure yet. I want to get back to our condo, get some rest, and I'll tell you in the morning."

Robbie turned away and looked out the side window but didn't like what he was hearing from Steve.

The Sims and the Lawrences woke up around 8:00 Saturday morning. They had a lot of packing to do before they checked out. They also were anticipating Chief Graham's call. Everyone was very anxious to help in any way they could to catch these two guys and anyone who might be involved with their criminal activity.

"I hate this week is over," Coco commented.

"Me, too, Coco. It's been so much fun." Courtney replied.

Ralph's cell rang, and it was the Chief. After placing it on speaker mode, he spoke. "This is Ralph."

"Ralph, it's Graham. Are you ready to make the call to the station?"

"Yessir. I've written down what I'm going to say."

"Good. Make the call and then have one of the other adults call me at the same time. That way, I'll know for sure that the desk Officer is talking to you. Understand?"

"Got it," Ralph replied.

Ralph told Tim to get ready to call the Chief, and Ralph made the call. Tim followed suit and called the Chief. Graham answered, and he kept Tim on the phone as he watched and listened to the Desk Officer.

"Sugar Sands Police Station. May I help you?" The desk Officer answered as he usually did.

Ralph began. "Yes, I'd like to speak to Chief Graham or Officer Watson if either is in."

"And what is this concerning?"

"An ongoing investigation concerning two men who have been considered as the suspects who have been breaking and entering in various condos."

"Hold, please."

Graham was watching the desk Chief to see how he would respond to Ralph's request. The desk Officer put the call on hold, placed the receiver down, retrieved his cell phone, typed something, and returned to the call after a couple of minutes.

"I'm sorry, both the Chief and Officer Watson are unavailable. Would you like me to take down your message, and I can dispatch it to them?"

"Please. It's quite important. Tell them we were at Alvin's at the corner of Hwy 59 and spotted the individuals they have been looking for."

"Okay, I'll dispatch this to them ASAP. Anything else?"

"No, sir. Thank you."

After the desk Officer finished his call, Graham noticed that he grabbed his cell again and typed something. He was curious if he was typing notes to himself or was texting someone. What he didn't do was dispatch Ralph's call to them, which was not surprise.

"Tim, thank you and Ralph for your assistance this morning. Hopefully, this will help us in getting some answers. I'll let you know more as this continues to unfold."

"Thank you, Chief," Tim responded.

"Well, Ralph spoke. I guess all we can do now is wait."

"Yep, and pray, of course," Tim added.

"Absolutely! Let's finish packing the vehicle."

They had to be out of their condo by 11:00 a.m., and it was only 9:30, so they had plenty of time to pack and tidy up the place so they wouldn't be charged any additional cleaning fees.

"As I said before, Melinda spoke as she was putting the sheets and towels into the washer. I hate this part of any trip."

"I know. Me, too." Vicki agreed as she was putting dishes into the dishwasher.

Coco and Courtney asked if there was anything else they needed to help with, but there was nothing. They asked if it was okay to go outside until they left. Their moms said that would be fine, just don't get all sandy and dirty. They went outside and went down to the pool area. Before reaching the pool, both girls were seized by the two so-called pre-med students. They had been hanging around their condo, hoping to capitalize on an opportunity to grab them. They placed their hands over the girl's mouths, carried them to their truck, and threw them into the backseat of the cab. Ralph and Tim had just entered the elevator at the exact moment to retrieve more luggage, barely missing the altercation.

The girls screamed as loudly as they could while Robbie fought off their wrestling. The back doors were locked, so the girls couldn't open them.

"Shut up, you two. Do you see this?" Steve held up a pistol, and they quieted down and suddenly stopped any other movements.

Robbie looked at Steve and exclaimed. "I didn't know you had a gun. Where'd you get that?"

"Don't worry about it," Steve answered.

Robbie was perplexed. He didn't know what Steve was planning, and he sure didn't like it.

"I don't know your plans, Steve, but I don't want any part of this."

"Well, you are already part of it, so you might as well put your big boy pants on and do what I say."

He pulled into a convenience store with gas pumps and told Robbie. "Now, listen, bonehead, I'm gotta get some gas and some cigarettes. You keep the gun on them and keep them quiet."

He stepped out of the truck, placed the gas nozzle into the gas tank, and went inside the store to get his cigarettes.

Robbie took that moment, unlocked the back doors, looked at the girls, and spoke. "Hurry up. Get out and run."

The Courtneys didn't waste a minute and took advantage of the good fortune Robbie was showing them. As they were running away, they noticed he, too, was doing the same in the opposite direction.

Steve walked back to his empty vehicle and cursed. Under his breath, he said. "I'll find you, Robbie, and kick your ever-living butt. You're an idiot!"

He jerked the gas pump out of the tank, jumped into the driver's seat, and sped off, looking for Robbie and the girls.

Tim asked Vicki and Melinda if they were ready to get going. They both needed another fifteen minutes to ensure the condo was in good enough shape so they could leave.

Melinda told Ralph. "Why don't you tell the girls we're about to leave, and if they need to use the restroom, this would be the time to go."

"Where are they?" Ralph asked.

"They wanted to go outside and goof off before we left. We thought they would be at the pool or the shoreline. You didn't see them while you were loading the vehicle?"

"No," Ralph answered while looking toward the shoreline.

Melinda commented. "They wouldn't have gone very far because they left their cell phones on the kitchen table."

Tim said to Ralph. "Come on, let's go find them."

Tim and Ralph rode the elevator to the bottom floor, checked the pool area, and didn't see them. They then looked over the beach area directly behind their condo. No Courtneys. They looked up and down the beach, but there was no sight of them anywhere. They walked back toward the pool and heard some shouting over and over.

"Dad!" That got their attention really quickly.

"Where have you two been?" Ralph inquired with some angst in his voice.

The girls proceeded to tell them what had happened. Immediately, Ralph pulled out his cell and called Chief Graham's personal cell number.

"Graham here."

"Chief. This is Ralph Sims. Our daughters were abducted a few minutes ago by those two thugs."

"What?"

"While one of them went into the store to pay for their gas, the other one released our girls." "Please, Mr. Sims, slow down. I'm not quite understanding your story."

Ralph caught his breath and slowed down enough so the Chief could understand what he was telling him.

"Do the girls know which convenience store they stopped at?"

Ralph turned his speaker on. "Chief Graham, this is Courtney. The convenience store was the one across from Sam's Sandwich Shoppe."

"Got it. So, how long did it take you two to get back to your condo."

Coco answered. "We've been back for about fifteen minutes."

"Did either of you happen to see which direction their truck went?"

Coco responded. "No, sir. As soon as the one, called Robbie let us go, we ran as hard as we could to get back here. We saw him jump and run, too. We just don't know where."

At that moment, Chief Graham received a call from Officer Watson. "Excuse me. Officer Watson is calling. Can I put you on hold?" He didn't wait for a reply.

"Whatcha need, Watson?"

"You're never gonna believe this, but guess who walked into the police station a few minutes ago?"

"Watson, I don't have time for any guessing games. I'm on the other line with the Sims and Lawrences and…"

Watson interrupted, "And they are telling you about their girls getting kidnapped this morning by those two thugs."

"How'd you know that?"

"That's what I was trying to tell you. One of the guys who did it just walked in and turned himself in. He told me who he was, what had just occurred, and all about the various criminal activities he and this other guy have been involved in."

Chief Graham asked Officer Watson, "What about the other clown? Does he know where he is?"

"No, sir. He might be at the vacant condo they'd been staying in or maybe headed to Pensacola?"

"Pensacola? Why there?"

"He said that's where they fence their stolen goods."

"Wow! This guy is really spilling his guts."

"Yep. You won't believe all the information. I put out an APB for everyone to be on the lookout for the Tacoma. Maybe we'll get lucky and catch him before he gets too far. By the way, I asked Officer Williams to take a drive to the vacant condo they'd been living in, but there was no sign of the other one. Why don't you come back to the station, and we'll try and sort out more of this stuff."

"Sounds good. Be there in a few."

The Chief informed the Sims and Lawrences of the exciting news Officer Watson had just told him.

"Great news, Chief," Tim remarked.

"Yes, it is. I'm going back to the station now to see what else we can find. You all have a safe trip back, and again, thank you for all your assistance."

They said their goodbyes, and as the Chief was driving away, the Sims and Lawrence families got into their, packed to the brim, SUV headed back to Jackson, Mississippi.

"Another eventful vacation for the Sims and the Lawrences, wouldn't you say?" Tim quipped.

"That's putting it mildly," Melinda answered.

"Why don't we stay another week?" Courtney asked jokingly.

"Yeah! One more week would be great." Coco agreed.

"I don't think I could stand any more of the stress." Vicki jokingly replied.

They all chuckled and settled in for the five-hour trip, not counting restroom breaks.

CHAPTER NINE: SCARY STUFF

Chief Graham pulled into his designated parking spot at the police station. Officer Watson saw him come in the front door and waved him into his office.

"I've got the perp that surrendered in the interrogation room. He's cooperating to the fullest. He said he got scared when the other guy pulled out a gun. He says he didn't even know he owned one. To be honest, Chief, he seems a little slow, if you know what I mean?"

"Let's go see him."

They walked down the hall and around the corner into the room. Watson had bought him some lunch, and he was almost finished. Graham shook Robbie's hand.

"I'm Chief Graham. Officer Watson told me that you have been very complicit and forthright with the details concerning you and your partner's activities. I appreciate you turning yourself in. The judge will perhaps give that strong consideration when this goes to court."

"Well, sir, I would sincerely appreciate that, but actually, I'm just ready to do my time and start all over as soon as I can. I know I've been doing wrong, but I just couldn't get away from it."

"We understand, son. We're going to put you into a cell and begin proceedings for your crimes. You'll find out later how much your bail will be."

Robbie looked like a poor puppy dog and said, "Sir, I ain't got no money for anything, much less for bail. I've been in jail before. I'll be okay there. It's probably the safest place for me right now, anyway. Not sure what Steve would do if he found me."

The Chief sat there for a few moments and didn't say anything. He just stared up toward the ceiling and asked Watson to step outside with him. "We'll be back, son."

"I have an idea, Watson. Robbie has Steve's contact on his phone, correct?"

"I supposed so," Watson responded.

"We could use this to our advantage in a big way."

"How so, Chief?"

"If Robbie would be willing to help us, we could drop him off at a location in our city, have him call his buddy, and tell him he's sorry he ran out on him. He'll tell him he was just scared and ask him to come get him. We, of course, would be waiting for him."

Watson took his hat off and scratched his bald head. After a moment, he said. "I believe this could work, Chief. You think Robbie could pull it off?"

"That's the unknown, but I think it's worth a try. Come on."

The Officers returned to the interrogation room and proceeded to explain their plan to Robbie and gave him a minute to assimilate it.

After a long pause, Robbie opened up to the Officers and spoke. "You know, I ain't done too many things right while I've been on this earth. This is something I could do to make a difference, ain't it?"

"Well, son, the Chief replied, it very well could. You'd be helping to put away what seems to be a potential career criminal."

"You talking about Steve?"

"Of course."

"He can be okay most of the time. It's just lately, he's gotten all out of whack."

Officer Watson offered, "Robbie, sometimes people get out of whack, as you call it, and start hurting other people. We're afraid that's the road Steve has chosen."

Robbie looked down at the floor, wringing his hands, and finally said. "I'll do whatever I can do to help."

"Thank you, Robbie. Here's what we are going to do."

The Chief proceeded to tell Robbie the scheme, hopefully allowing them to apprehend his partner.

On the way out, the Sims and Lawrences decided to get their last really fresh seafood fix, so they went to lunch at Skullys. It was a real favorite in Sugar Sands for the locals, as well as the vacationers. It was famous for its delicious hush puppies, popcorn shrimp, and their shrimp po'boys. Kids loved it because the restaurant was shaped to look like an old pirate ship. In fact, some stairs wound up toward a wooden plank about twenty feet off the floor. For a few dollars, if one wanted a souvenir of eating there, a Skully's pirate, holding a fake sword, would walk you onto it and then push you into a large inflatable ring full of soft plastic balls. Another employee dressed up like one of Skully's pirates would take a picture of the experience and have it for you before you finished your dinner. Of course, both Courtneys did it.

Steve, the other criminal, had driven back toward the condo and watched the Lawrences and Sims pulling out of the parking lot. He was hoping to get another chance to seize the girls for some ransom money. Now, he would just have to be patient and wait for the right time, and it had to be perfect.

"At least I won't have to contend with that bonehead, Robbie, to mess up my plan." Steve thought to himself.

They pulled into Skully's Restaurant, but he passed by. He didn't want them to recognize his truck. He did a U-turn, went back to the restaurant, and parked his vehicle. He then walked into the restaurant and went to the bar with his ballcap pulled down tight. He saw the two families that he'd been stalking. Now, he had to wait until he could grab at least one of the two brats.

He was startled by his cell phone ringing. He looked at the ID and saw it was his sorry partner in crime who messed everything up.

"What do you want, idiot? You run out on me right with the best money-making scheme I've ever had, but guess what, moron? I'll be taking home all the dough, and you'll still be left working for pennies. Cya, clown."

"Wait, Steve. Don't hang up, man. I got scared. I've never seen you with a gun, and I didn't know what you were planning on doing with those girls. I ran scared, that's all. Come get me. I promise I won't do that again."

"Nope. No way. You showed your true colors. You're a real loser, and I don't want to have any part with losers like you."

"Steve, I messed up, man. I messed up big time. Please pick me up. I want it to be like it used to be. Please!"

Chief Graham and Officer Watson were extremely impressed with Robbie's fortitude and courage to play this role.

"Forget it, fool. I ain't got time for you anymore. I might call you once I get to the Bahamas, where I'll be living large, just to remind you just how bad you screwed up."

"Steve, come on, man. Give me another chance. I don't have any other place to turn."

"You should have thought about it before you bailed on me."

Steve, ple.."

Click. Steve was gone. Little did he know that the police had tapped his phone as he was talking. They got to his location and swiftly rushed to Skully's restaurant.

Steve saw both girls leaving their tables and going to the restroom. They literally walked right behind him. He would need a distraction so people wouldn't notice him grabbing one of them. Next to him were two obnoxious guys at the bar who had more to drink than they should. Earlier, the bartender had already asked them to quiet down, but they just got progressively louder and louder. Steve would use this to his advantage. As soon as the girls walked out, he would shove one of them into the other, which hopefully would cause a ruckus between them. If the plan wouldn't work, he'd have to think of another. He was too close to his monetary plan working, and he wasn't going to let this opportunity slip by.

The girls stepped out of the restroom, and Steve put his plan into motion. He shoved the patron beside him, who was drinking his alcoholic beverage hard enough to almost knock the other fellow off his seat. Both men stood up with their drinks all over their shirts and started yelling at each other. The Courtneys stopped at that moment so they wouldn't be in the middle of the altercation, and Steve took the opportunity to grab one of them and ran outdoors. He had taken Coco. It caught Courtney so much by surprise that she stood there for a moment, wondering what was happening. She thought at first the man had grabbed Coco to keep her from getting hurt, but then, she immediately recognized him and yelled at the top of her lungs, "He's got Coco. The parents were already facing that way because of all the commotion that was coming from the bar area and saw her waving at them to follow her. Ralph and Tim jumped up from their seats, pushed customers out of the way, and followed her outside. Vicki and Melinda were right behind them. When they got outside, Coco was running toward them. Chief Graham and Officer Watson were placing handcuffs onto the thug's wrists while four or five squad vehicles were in the background, their blue lights brightly shining. It would be a long time before he attempts to kidnap anyone else or do anything else nefarious.

"Are you okay, hon?" Vicki asked while hugging Coco.

"Yes, ma'am. I'm okay."

Courtney grabbed her best friend and gave her a big bear hug.

"I'm so glad you're okay." Courtney told her.

"Me, too, Court."

"Tim, Ralph, I really need you all to come back to the station so I can get your statements for our report. Can you do that for me?" Chief Graham asked.

Both said in agreement that they would be glad to. They all followed the two Officers to the police station. It only took an hour or so until each one of them gave their statements to the Officers. Chief Graham thanked them for their time and then asked.

"Do you all know where the Gulf Star Resort is?"

They all nodded yes. It was probably the most recognized and most remarkable resort in the Sugar Sands area.

"Well, if you would allow us the privilege, the city would like to put you there for the night."

Tim looked at Ralph, Vicki, and Melinda, saw the amazement on their faces, and answered, "Chief, we're overwhelmed with your offer and very grateful."

"Great. When you arrive, tell them who you are. We have reserved their presidential suite for you all. Also, enjoy supper tonight at their 5-star restaurant.. It also will be on the city's tab."

"Wow! Reservations at the Gulf Star and supper in their finest restaurant. We are so incredibly grateful." Vicki remarked.

"Well, we wanted to show our appreciation for all the assistance you all have given in the apprehension of these two criminals."

Everyone thanked both Officers, especially for all they did to catch those two public menaces. They left the station and drove to the Gulf Star.

They booked Steve, put him into one of their cells, and saw Robbie in another. Robbie was schooled earlier on what to do when Steve saw him.

Steve, not surprised, said to Robbie, "So, they caught you, too."

"Yeah. Since you wouldn't come get me after I called, I didn't know what I was gonna do. I had to find a way to make some money so I could get out of town. I went into an ice cream shop, acted like I had a gun, and robbed the pimple-faced kid behind the counter. I got a big whopping twenty-eight dollars. The kid must have called the cops and given them my description because it wasn't, but after a few minutes, some cops saw me walking down Highway 59 and threw me into his vehicle."

"You truly are an idiot," Steve replied.

Robbie looked down at the gray cement floor with a dejected expression on his face, still playing his role.

"I'll try to get us outta this mess. Just don't be so stupid next time."

Robbie looked up and nodded.

Chief Graham spoke. "Watson, got a minute?"

"Sure. What's up?"

"We still have a problem."

Watson knew exactly what he was referring to.

"Yeah, I was gonna bring it up to you later, as well. How do we go about it?"

"I think we ask him to meet us in my office, and we point blank ask him why we were left out of the loop on those calls and how he is involved."

"Let's do it, Chief."

"An indoor pool! Look at the waterfall coming off that huge rock formation. This is unbelievable!" Coco hollered.

"I know. It's awesome!" Courtney shouted in agreement. "I'm headed for the water tube slide."

"I'm right behind you," Coco responded.

"Looks like the girls are having an exciting time. Sure, I'm glad things turned out like they did. There were a couple of scary moments, to say the least." Vicki said to Melinda.

"Seriously, Vic. God has been so good and gracious watching and protecting our families."

"Amen, Mel."

"No, you didn't!" Melinda screamed.

Ralph and Tim both, not using their best judgment, jumped into the pool at the same time and splashed pool water all over their wives. Vicki and Melinda weren't totally drenched, but they had a fair amount of wetness all over them.

Vicki then threw out a promise. "Well, boys, you can bet on one thing. That little fun you had at our expense will eventually come back to haunt you. You'll not know when, what, or where, but our payback will be incredible."

"We were just having a little fun," Tim replied.

"Yeah. We didn't mean to get you that wet." Ralph semi-apologized.

"No, no, no, boys. We're fine. Just be sure to watch your back. You never know when retribution will come upon you." Melinda said assuredly.

Vicki and Melinda then slapped their hands together with a high five. Tim and Ralph swam backward, motioning to their wives that they were sorry. Vicki and Melinda just looked at them with an assured smile, which worried their husbands tremendously. The Courtneys saw the whole ordeal and swam to their respective dads.

"Y'all really messed up, Dad," Coco said to Tim.

"Yep. Not the wisest thing I've ever seen you do, Dad." Courtney told her dad.

The girls and their dads had an enjoyable time playing in the pool while Vicki and Melinda went to the room to dry off and get ready to go to dinner. The ladies never really got mad about the incident. In fact, they thought it was funny. But, of course, they were going to keep Tim or Ralph wondering how their little prank would affect the rest of the evening.

Chief Graham and Officer Watson called Officer Shift, the Desk Officer, into the Chief's office and started their interrogation.

"So, Shift, tell Officer Watson and me why we never received knowledge of any calls or information about these two perps we just brought in?"

He hesitated for a second without making any eye contact with either one of them and then answered.

"Well, sir, I'm really not sure I'm at liberty to say."

"Shift, I'm the Chief of this police department, and you answer directly to me. So, it probably would behoove you to answer my question."

"Yessir, but…"

The Chief quickly barked back. "There ain't no but's about it, Shift. Answer my question, or I'll write you up for insubordination."

Shift sat there and chewed his bottom lip until you thought it was going to bleed, and then he opened up.

"I'd been told not to let you two know about the calls."

"Why and who told you not to let us know."

"The assistant Mayor, Mr. Stevens. He said that you two were under a secret investigation. He said there were suspicions that you were involved with those two guys."

"What? Mr. Stevens told you we were crooked?"

"I don't know about all that. All I know is he told me every time I get a call about those two thugs, I was to text him and make sure you two never heard about the calls."

"Wow? Can you believe this, Chief?" Watson asked with amazement.

The Chief just rolled his eyes and gave a slight chuckle.

The Chief continued. "Shift, don't you realize that he nor the Mayor have any authority over you and your employment with the police station?"

"Well, Chief, in all due respect, Mr. Stevens said if I didn't cooperate with them and you two were found guilty, I could be considered an accessory."

"How long have you known me, Shift?"

"Ever since I've been on the force, sir. Six years."

"Have I, and for that matter, Watson, given you any reason to think we would be on the take, or we could be crooked cops?"

Shift looked down at the painted cement floor and then slowly looked up and answered the Chief.

"No sir, no reason at all. I feel pretty stupid. I guess I should have come and talked to ya."

The Chief hesitated, took a look at Watson, then proceeded to tell Shift how he was going to assist in clearing up all this mess. Watson looked at his cell phone, excused himself, and said he had to take care of a situation and he'd be back in a minute.

The Sim's and Lawrence's dinner reservations were for 8:00 sharp. They stepped into the elevator and saw that the five-star restaurant was perched on the highest floor possible—the twenty-fifth floor.

Tim leaned in and punched the number twenty-five. They all stood patiently and waited for the elevator to reach its destination. Tim shifted next to Ralph and whispered.

"Vicki didn't seem upset at all when we got back from the pool. I thought for sure she was going to say something."

"Mel didn't either. That's not like her. Maybe they saw how we were just trying to have some fun, and they are okay with it."

Tim gave Ralph a look that said he didn't necessarily believe that.

The elevator finally stopped, the doors opened, and Coco was the first to make a comment.

"Swanky!".

Courtney said while pointing to the right. "Look at the huge indoor aquarium. It even has a couple of sharks swimming around in there."

The maître d' welcomed them and then walked them to their table. The table sat next to the window, and the view was nothing short of spectacular. They could see the shoreline of the beach, varied dots of lights in the gulf of different watercraft, and the glimmering reflection of the moon on the water. The scene looked like a magazine cover and couldn't be more beautiful if one had planned it. The whole dining experience was something they would never forget, and they were extremely grateful for the privilege. They all agreed to make sure they sent a thank you card to Chief Graham.

Watson entered back into the Chief's office. "Get it handled?" Chief Graham asked. "Yessir. It wasn't a big deal."

Shift wondered what they were talking about but didn't ask any questions.

"Shift, the Chief began. Does the assistant Mayor or anyone in the Mayor's office know about the arrest of these men?"

"No sir, well, at least I haven't told them."

"Well, here's what you're gonna do. You're going to make a call to Mr. Stevens and tell him that the perps were caught, brought in by me and Watson, and were placed into a holding cell. Tell him we were going to start interrogating them, but we received another call and had to go check it out. At that point, ask him what he wants you to do."

"What do you think he'll do, Chief?"

"We're not really sure, but we're going to have to be prepared for anything. Officer Watson is going to be outside in his personal vehicle, and I'll be in this other office. Shift, he can't know we're here, understand?"

"Yessir."

"You just play along, and we'll handle the rest."

"Yessir."

You could tell Officer Shift was quite nervous about the entire charade but was more than willing to help.

Shift made the call to the assistant Mayor's personal cell since it was after hours.

Mr. Stevens answered. "What do you want, Shift?"

"Sir, I figured you'd want to know this. Chief Graham and Officer Watson just brought in those two guys."

Mr. Stevens sat up and put his recliner into its sitting position and asked Shift. "Where are the guys now?"

"They're in separate holding cells."

"What about the Chief and Watson."

"They had to answer another call and said they'd be back to interrogate them."

"Shift, don't let anyone get near them. I'm coming over there right now. Take the two men out of their cells and place them together in one of the interrogation rooms. Now!"

The assistant Mayor took the bait. He put on some jeans, a polo shirt, and deck shoes, then drove as fast as his Lexus would go to the station. The traffic lights were kind, and he arrived within thirty minutes. Watson saw him pull in and walk up the stairs to the front door. The Chief was in a side office standing with the door cracked just enough to see out, but no one could see him.

"Where are they, Shift?"

"Back in room two, sir."

Shift walked directly to the room and shut the door. Officer Shift went back to the lobby desk.

"Steve immediately asked him who he was and what he wanted.

"I'm the one who kept you two from getting caught and thrown in jail a lot earlier. Alright, look you, clowns. You've really messed up. We don't have much time, so here's what you're gonna do. You're gonna yell out to the desk Officer that he's gotta come back here quick. Shout out that it looks like I'm having a heart attack. When he walks in, he'll see me on the floor as if I've been hit. Steve, you'll be behind the door, and you'll grab his gun."

"I ain't sure I can do this."

Steve threw his left elbow into Robbie's ribs. "Shut up, you idiot. We're gettin' outta here. Do what we tell you to do."."

Steve had hit him so hard Robbie was having a tough time breathing.

Mr. Stevens looked at him and spoke. "Robbie, I don't have time for your stupidity. You'll do what I'm telling you, or I make sure your sweet little momma in Pensacola encounters some kind of fatal accident. Understand?"

Robbie didn't know what to say or do, so he kept his mouth shut. He thought maybe he could do something later to foil their plan. The assistant Mayor continued telling them how the plan would work.

"When Officer Shift comes in, and you have his gun, tell him to unlock your cuffs. Lock him and me in the room, and after a while, I'll slowly get up and tell him you two jumped me, and I must have been temporarily knocked out. I'll meet you later at the old amusement place called Paradise Fun off of Paradise Ave."

It was time to put their plan into action.

Steve hollered. "Officer Shift! This guy is having a heart attack or seizure or something."

After Shift got the okay from the Chief, he ran to the back room. It all happened just like they had hoped. Before the two guys ran out of the police station, they found the location where their truck keys were kept. The Chief had made sure the key box was unlocked. They grabbed them, went out the front door, found their truck, and drove away. Watson, of course, followed them in his personal vehicle so as not to draw attention or suspicion. The desk Officer had a key to the locked interrogation room door, opened it, and he and Mr. Stevens left the room.

He told Officer Shift. "I'm going after them." Don't tell anyone about this. Do you hear me?"

Officer answered, "Yessir!"

The assistant Mayor hurriedly left the lobby and got into his city vehicle. The Chief stepped out of the office where he was hidden and told Officer Shift that he handled everything perfectly.

"Thank you, sir. Do I need to put out an APB about the escape convicts?"

"Not right now. Me and Officer Watson have things in play that hopefully will allow us to quickly apprehend them again. I'll call you if I see the need for it later."

With that, the Chief left the police station, jumped into his personal vehicle, and started his pursuit after Mr. Stevens. The Chief was hoping that Mr. Stevens would lead them directly to the perps. If not, the other part of the plan should do the job.

On the way to the Lawrence's and Sim's rooms, they walked through the gorgeous atrium filled with thousands of beautiful flowers and plants. All that beauty surrounded the spectacular indoor pool that the two Courtneys enjoyed earlier and where Ralph's and Tim's prank didn't fare very well.

"Hey, everybody, let's get a picture standing by the pool with the waterfall in the background." Melinda requested.

"Great idea, Mel. This will make for a great memory." Vicki replied.

Everyone gathered together in formation. Tim and Ralph were together with their wives on each side and Coco and Courtney on each end. It was going to be a perfect picture. Melinda held out her selfie stick with her cell phone on the end and set the timer for ten seconds.

"Alright, ready, everybody?" All said yes. Ten, nine, eight, seven, six, five, four, three, and on two, Vicki and Melinda shoved their husbands, clothes and all, into the pool. Sploosh! They shot up out of the water and looked in shock at their wives.

Vicki and Melinda said in unison. "Oh, we're so sorry. We didn't mean to get you that wet."

Tim and Ralph just looked at each other and said they had definitely been beaten by the best. The Courtneys couldn't catch their breath they were laughing so hard. Tim and Ralph finally yielded to the queens of pranks.

Tim then said, "You all should join us. The water feels great."

To their husband's amazement, Melinda, Vicki, and the Courtneys started taking off their dresses.

Tim and Ralph both said, "What are you four doing? Stop!"

Little did the husbands know, they had their bathing suits underneath their clothes. They jumped into the pool, and both families had the time of their lives.

CHAPTER ELEVEN: THE CHASE

The chase was on. Chief Graham was following the assistant Mayor and Officer Watson was already on the tail of the two escaped thieves. Earlier, when Officer Watson said he had a situation he had to handle, he attached a tracker to the back bumper of their Tacoma, making it easier for him to trail their truck too closely. The Chief had to be a little more careful since they didn't have the opportunity to place one on Mr. Stevens' car. "Watson, can you hear me?"

"Yes, sir."

The Chief and Watson communicated on a separate channel so others couldn't hear them.

The Chief continued. "Mr. Stevens took the bait, and I'm assuming he's meeting with the two criminals at an agreed location."

"Yes sir, I'm thinking that, too. Chief, they're slowing down, and it looks like they're pulling into an old, abandoned amusement area off Paradise Avenue. Paradise Fun."

The Chief told Watson he knew that place and to find a place to park where he wouldn't be seen and wait for him and also keep a lookout for the assistant Mayor's vehicle.

Shortly after the Chief's and Officer Watson's last conversation, Mr. Stevens pulled into the amusement park parking lot. Officer Watson was close enough to watch him drive around to the back through a gate that had a sign, Maintenance entrance. He assumed that was where the two escapees were, as well.

"Watson, where are you?"

"Across the street at the Dollar General store."

"I see you."

Chief Graham parked his car next to Watson's and waved at him to get into his vehicle. Officer Watson shut the car door and sat down in the passenger seat. "Chief, what's our next move?"

"Not sure. Where did they go when they pulled in?"

"Through the maintenance gate on the left."

The Chief thought for a moment.

"If our plan is going to work, we need to catch all three of them together. Do you think we can trust Officer Williams?"

"I've known Butch ever since I've been on the force. He's always been straight up, as far as I know."

"I feel the same way. Give him a call. Tell him we need some backup and that we are going on into the maintenance area to see if we can find them."

"Yessir."

Watson immediately called Officer Williams, and he said he'd be there within twenty minutes. "He said he'd be here in twenty minutes."

Chief Graham told Watson that they needed to move.

With that, the Chief backed out of his parking spot and drove across to the front of the amusement entrance, right next to a neglected garbage bin so his car wouldn't be seen. They stepped out, pistols drawn, and walked through the maintenance gate. They saw both Tacoma and Mr. Steven's Lexus.

"Watson, Chief Graham whispered to Watson, deflate the front tire on the truck, and I'll do the same on the Lexus just in case they're able to give us the slip."

After doing that, they ambled toward the door that led to the maintenance shop. They opened it very slowly. The bottom floor was not lit very well, but the upstairs office was, and Graham and Watson could see all three men. Watson took out his cell phone and took a couple of pictures to document their meeting. They gradually approached the stairs and began quietly climbing them step by step. Once they stepped onto the top landing, they were about five feet from the office door. They stopped and listened carefully. Watson made sure his cell was recording every word.

They heard Mr. Stevens talking.

"Look, you clowns. I don't want any more arguments from you. I don't care that you don't have any money. That's on you. You're the idiots that messed up, not me."

One of the men argued back. "But Mr. Stevens, we gotta have money just to get outta town like you want us to."

Mr. Stevens let out a string of expletives that would make the most hardened criminal blush and then said.

"Look, here's fifty bucks. You leave and don't ever come back, and don't ever think about contacting me. You do, and you both will have an early funeral. I'll make sure of it."

Their meeting abruptly ended when they heard something downstairs. Officer Williams had opened the maintenance shop door a little too quickly, and it made a slight unintended squeal.

Mr. Stevens and the two men stepped outside, and they spotted Chief Graham and Officer Watson. The escapee, Steve, charged the Chief. The Chief lowered his body, lifted the first one off his feet, and tossed him over the railing. He fell awkwardly and broke his left arm and left leg. Watson grabbed Mr. Stevens and told him he was under arrest while Robbie stood out of the way.

"What do you mean, under arrest? I was undercover the whole time, trying to catch these guys. I demand you uncuff me now. If you don't, I'll have your badge."

Watson looked at the assistant Mayor and calmly told him his Miranda rights, smiling like a Cheshire cat at the same time. The Chief cuffed Robbie and quietly told him he was going to do everything he could to help him since he'd been so helpful.

"Thank you very much, Chief, but I deserve everything I get." Robbie said humbly.

The Chief walked Robbie downstairs as Watson did the same with Mr. Stevens as he continued to scream and yell obscenities at them.

Officer Williams apologized for being so loud coming through the door while picking up Steve from the floor. Steve shrieked, complaining about the severe pain, but Officer Williams didn't seem to have much compassion, which was fine with the Chief and Officer Watson. The Chief called Officer Shift and told him to send a vehicle to their location so all three could have a nice time with each other on their way to the police station.

CHAPTER TWELVE: GOING HOME

Sunday morning at 9:00, the Sims and Lawrences were already packed. They grabbed a quick bite at Hardee's and then dropped by City Hope Church for their morning service, which started at 10:15.

"I hope Anne is singing a solo this morning again," Coco commented.

"Well, I'm sure Ralph is hoping to see the 3-B one more time." Tim snorted.

They all chuckled except Ralph and gave Tim the stink eye. They walked into the lobby, and sure enough, the Bama Beach Bum was there, and he and Anne both had welcoming duty.

"Good morning, y'all. Matthew said. Glad to have you joining us again, but I thought you all were leaving yesterday."

Ralph offered, "Well, we were, but a couple of things happened, and well, here we are."

Anne remarked, "We're very glad to have you."

"Miss Anne, Coco asked, are you singing another solo today?"

"No, Coco. The gentleman with the long hair you might have noticed last week is doing the solo work today."

You could see the disappointment on Coco's face, but she understood.

"And how are you and Courtney doing?" Anne asked.

Both answered, "Doing great, Miss Anne."

Tim looked at the families and spoke. "Guess we better find a seat. It seems to be filling up quickly."

They found some seats together on the fourth row and thoroughly enjoyed the worship experience.

They were walking out the front door, and Matthew called out to Ralph.

"Y'all give us a shout next time you're in this area. We'd love to hear from you."

"Thanks much, Matthew. We'll sure do it."

The girls waved at Anne, and she said, "See y'all next time. Have a safe trip."

Melinda wrapped her arm around Ralph and jokingly asked. "Are you gonna be okay, honey?"

This time, Ralph gave her the stink eye as everyone was laughing. Before Tim stepped into the Sim's SUV, his cell phone rang. It was Chief Graham.

"Hope I didn't catch you at an inconvenient time, but I thought you would want to know about the most recent happenings with our investigation."

Tim put his speaker mode on, and the Chief proceeded to tell them all the good news. They were extremely thrilled, to say the least.

"Be safe on the road, and thank you again for all your help."

Tim replied. "And we thank you, Chief. Take care, and you be safe, as well."

Tim ended the call, and they all offered a prayer of thanksgiving to the Lord as they headed back home.

www.ingramcontent.com/pod-product-compliance
Lightning Source LLC
Chambersburg PA
CBHW030008010826
48973CB00009B/2714